INNER CITY

GIRL 2

Other Rivers to Cross

Colleen Smith-Dennis

LMH PUBLISHING LIMITED

Editor: K. Sean Harris
Cover Illustration: Courtney Lloyd Robinson
Cover Design: Roshane Anglin
Book Design, Layout & Typesetting: Roshane Anglin

Published by LMH Publishing Limited
Suite 10-11, Sagicor Industrial Park
7 Norman Road
Kingston C.S.O., Jamaica
Tel.: 876-938-0005; 876-938-0712
Fax: 876-759-8752
Email: lmhbookpublishing@cwjamaica.com
Website: www.lmhpublishing.com

Printed in the U.S.A.   ISBN: 978-976-8245-67-0

NATIONAL LIBRARY OF JAMAICA CATALOGUING-IN-PUBLICATION DATA

Smith-Dennis, Colleen
      Inner city girl 2 : other rivers to cross / Colleen Smith-Dennis.

      p. ; cm

ISBN 978-976-8245-67-0 (pbk)

1. Teenage girls – Jamaica – Juvenile fiction
2. Social classes – Juvenile fiction
3. Jamaican fiction
I. Title

813   dc 23

To my father.

All those who are left behind have found him faithful.

OTHER RIVERS TO CROSS

The pain, the shame, the blame seemed resolved.
Non-acceptance, exclusion, peripheral behaviour, all conquered.
Achievement, acceptance, mended walls, all featured.
The rivers had all been crossed, bridges all accessible, or so it seemed.
But the silent waters under the bridge rose in muddy spate.
They gained strength and threatened to drown as they murmured in a guttural voice, "It's not over, there are other rivers to cross."

One

Martina heard the beep on her cell phone and ignored it for a while. The network was always sending trivial messages about all kinds of things that did not interest her. Sometimes she rushed to read the messages and found it a waste of her valuable time. Let it stay there, she thought. I have more interesting things to think about and plan for.

She lay on the bed and looked around her. It was a capacious room, one that she had shared with her sister Yvette, for a little over two years. A ceiling fan and lamp graced the white gypsum ceiling; there were no brown stains revealing the constant intrusion of rain, which was such a marked difference between Martina's former home and this one. The walls were a restful yet bold cream and broad, cream ceramic tiles completed what for Martina was a grand room. Many times, she had looked around and marvelled at the change in her life occasioned by her mother's death and the wondrous discovery of a father she never knew she had. The bed she was lying on was devoid of lumps and torn patches. Lying on it was like sinking into soft, absorbing, soothing, soapy foam from a bubble bath which Martina had experienced only since she had come to live in Uppington Glade.

There were two double beds in the room which was so large that the girls still had space and did not feel crowded. The closet housed most of their clothes along with the huge dresser that they shared. The dresser was clean, smooth and soft brown unlike the scar-ridden chest of drawers which had been in their room in Dinsdale.

Martina rose from the bed and caught her face staring back from the mirror. She had not changed much, she mused, as she stared at the oval milo-complexioned face. The only change was that her face had gained a little more flesh and had filled out some of the hollows in her cheeks. Her face had refused to give up its saturnine look except on occasions when laughter blew out her cheeks and danced in her brooding eyes. Her hair was not natural anymore but had been processed and most times she wore it slicked down, caught up at the back in a banana clip. She only bothered to set it up when she had special occasions.

She got off the bed and surveyed herself in the closet mirror. She had no idea when she had grown as tall as five-feet-ten; for a female this could be considered tall. She concluded that this was something she had inherited from her over six-feet-tall father. She still had her mother's somewhat small bones but she was filling out gracefully and had often received unwelcomed glances from members of the opposite sex. Well, she told her appearance sternly, I have a goal to achieve and I am going to achieve it, comes what may, even if it is one day before I depart Mother Earth. My mother is dead, but she had a dream for me which I sanction and I am going to achieve it and go to her grave to show her my certificate, so boys stay clear until such time!

Beep, beep, beep, the phone invited her to pick it up. "Alright," she said aloud to the phone, "what trivia do you want me to waste my time with now?"

She picked up the phone and located the message. It was the same one twice. Her eyes widened with surprise and relief. She dashed through the room door and through the football-sized living room, almost hitting her great aunt's figurines and crystal from her what-not. She rushed through the dining room and the kitchen like an accelerated vehicle, imagining her aunt's scowl of disapproval if she had been there to see her.

"Miss Turner! Miss Turner! Yvette girl guess what?" She braked suddenly in front of the two, almost falling over. She reminded Miss Turner of someone suddenly stepping on brakes and screeching to a halt.

"Tina brake up properly, mine yuh car turn over!" Miss Turner exclaimed, stretching the myriads of crinkles which formed minute pleats on her blotchy face. The eyes which seemed to have receded farther and farther away with the passing years jumped to laughter from deep within. She looked at Martina as a proud mother would have looked on a daughter. A warm feeling of love sprang up inside her and spread within her body. She knew where this girl was coming from, the rivers she had crossed, the valleys she had traversed and the mountains she had climbed to get to this point. She exuded so much self-will and maturity that those around her had been encouraged by her attitude. How could one child who had been buffeted by the ill will of death, rejection and abduction, rally back and fight her way out of the quagmire of devastation and still remain focused?

"Anytime you act so excited it mus' be really something special!" Yvette exclaimed. She got up from the garden chair she had been sitting in and walked towards her sister. Even though her countenance was not as serious as Martina's she did not exactly wear a happy face. Her youthful exuberance had been crushed by an incestuous father. The scars were deeply etched in her being and only the passing of time and the intervention of fate could diminish them. Her brown face registered uneasiness and her eyes lacked fire.

"Guess what? Guess what? I got through for university and guess what again, I got through for mass communication!" she announced, asking and answering her own questions. She was beside herself with joy.

Miss Turner and Yvette like conjoined bodies moved towards her and hugged her, at first not saying a word and afterwards slapped her on the back and kissed her at the same time.

"But Tina gal why you behaving so surprised, with them

good grades and hard work I know you would get through. A tell you all along you mek for great things." Miss Turner beamed at her and then hobbled back to her seat, tears threatening to gush from her eyes. "Your mother would be really happy if she did live to see this day."

Martina's fluttering heart sobered. Her heart still felt sore at the mention of her mother, she had not recovered from her death and every time something good happened to her the wound opened a little more because her mother had wanted so badly for her to do well and move out of the inner city. Now she was on the verge of attending university and elation was too mild a word to describe how her mother would have felt, ecstatic would be closer to it.

Miss Turner watched the play of emotions on Martina's face. She knew exactly what was happening to her, after all Miss Fuller had been her friend too and she missed her a great deal despite her feisty ways and her mysterious, questionable behaviour. She had cared for her children and wanted the best for them. She was only too happy that she could deputize for her even though she could not fill her shoes. They had really needed a mother, especially Yvette who was so young and vulnerable.

"I have to call my father and tell him now. He is going to need time to find the school fee and everything else," Martina said, rushing inside to use the house phone.

Her father was elated. "Martina I knew they would have accepted you. Your lower sixth grades were excellent and you must have done well in that test you were given.

Congratulations again and go online to find out the rest of the details. I will come by later because I have to take my wife and everybody else to the airport. As I told you, they are going up for the summer and I am not certain what their plans are because they all have green cards. Your cousin Tian and his family are also going to the US as well. So, see you on my way back, bright sparks!" His pride for her acceptance could be heard in his voice.

Martina was still uncertain about her father, having not had him for more than fifteen years of her life, but he had played his role well since her mother's death, providing for her and putting a roof over her head at his aunt's house, taking her out of the inner city. She wasn't certain that his aunt wanted them there but at least she humoured her father. Martina, Yvette and Miss Turner did what they had to do and kept out of her way. She was in awe at living in such a big house, even if it was only two rooms at the back of the house, but Aunt Indra probably saw it as an imposition from people of such low social stature. Even though she did not say it, her eyes sometimes betrayed her smouldering annoyance.

Her grand-aunt's house was a huge one scorning the public thoroughfare by placing itself far from it. Huge ficus and aloof evergreen and palm trees stood guards along the spacious driveway and continued their duty around the road which circled the house, forming a kind of ring road. Green and flowering plants of all sizes and description resided in rectangular and circular beds surrounded by white picket fences which kept neatly shaven green grass in check. At the back of the house there were wooden seats under trees with superfluous leaves. Martina loved to sit, read and do her assignments in this tranquil setting.

The house itself was a magnificent edifice with fashionable columns and stone arches at the gate and the verandah and garage. The windows were darkened squares of glass seemingly designed to keep secrets. They were edged by a light metal frame. The rooms were large, especially the living room and Martina was convinced that if the heavy, ornately carved mahogany furniture were removed, it could be used as a form of football field. She had never sat in this room and only passed through occasionally.

She waited impatiently for her father and imagined that he was in every motor vehicle that sped by or slowed down. It was eleven o'clock when a car finally came zooming up the driveway. She would recognise the soft, steady purr of that well-oiled SUV engine anywhere. He did not come immediately to see her and she knew he had stopped to converse with his aunt.

When he knocked on the door, she opened it immediately, almost hitting him in the face. He was a tall man who still had his boyish figure. His eyes were small and dark and his nose was almost razor straight. His lips were thin and firmly set, hinting that he could be a strict man. A few grey hairs had popped up among the multitude of black ones, giving him the look of a man on his way to maturity.

He greeted his daughter in a cheerful yet nervous manner. "Hi Tina, my bright daughter. I am so proud of you, imagine making it in the competitive world of mass communication! So, we are going to have a journalist in the family! I know you will do well girl. Just put in your acceptance and I will take care of everything else."

Martina noticed his nervousness. His words were ones of cheer but his voice was dead and slightly tremulous and his hands when they touched her were slightly damp.

"Are you sick or something?" Martina asked looking at her father intently, purposefully, with concern in her voice. She always avoided saying daddy or father because she still felt as though she were feeling him out, assessing him, weighing his attitude and behaviour, trying to find out if he was just helping out because her mother was dead or if he was genuine.

He did not respond to her question and did not visit for long. He left saying he would call her the following day. He hurried out without greeting Yvette and Miss Turner who were in the other room watching television. Martina found this strange and wondered if his family leaving him alone for an undetermined amount of time had anything to do with his demeanour. She put her surmising out of her mind and went to bed, exulting in her acceptance and vowing to herself to graduate with top honours.

Next morning, she knocked at the kitchen door and called out to Aunt Indra. "Good morning, Aunt Indra," Martina said, struggling to pull out the weak, fake smile she always summoned when talking to her. She somehow managed to make Martina feel like a beggar who had landed in a privileged position. She never said a word, but her condescending look and manner made the sensitive Martina feel like a commoner in a queen's palace. Maybe she expected her to curtsy before she spoke to her. It was as if the many chores she saddled Martina and Yvette with were not enough to earn her respect. She had reduced the helper's workload from weekly to three days and divided up the work she would normally do between Martina and Yvette. It was Miss Turner who rescued them sometimes from preparing the dog food and cleaning out the kennel by telling the aunt they had many assignments to do. She seemed to dislike Miss Turner's visage and did not do much arguing with her.

When Martina told her good morning, she turned around reluctantly and mumbled good morning in return. Martina was all agog with her good news but Aunt Indra's aura daunted her somewhat. She was as fair as Miss Turner and she had long, deeply arched shaggy eyebrows with long lashes reaching towards her eyebrows. Her face was attractive but broad and flattened like flesh had been scraped from under it. She had a short neck which made swivelling around difficult, so she normally turned her body partially like an oscillating fan to respond to anyone who was talking to her. The size of her belly made up for both her buttocks and her belly. Her back was flat as if someone had deliberately, permanently kicked in her buttocks. In contrast, her shapely legs tapered down to small, delicate feet always shod in ballet shoes, reminiscent of her dancing days.

"Aunt Indra, I got through to do mass communication at University of the Caribbean for September," Martina said flatly, keeping the excitement out of her voice.

Aunt Indra looked at her blandly. "So you have, they have certainly watered down the matriculation, now just about anyone can get in." She swivelled back to whatever she was doing at the sink and totally ignored Martina.

When she thought about it later she could not decide why she had decided to address Aunt Indra's back. She found herself responding, "They did not do me a favour, the test was challenging and I have three ones and two twos in my CAPE subjects, in addition to my nine ones in the CXC exam and I am certain that my results in the other half of the CAPE will be good. I worked hard. I always work hard." She did not wait for her to swivel back but walked to her room, hot tears threatening to ruin her happiness. The impudence of that woman! To translate, she Martina Patterson was not good enough to attend a prestigious university! "I will show her," she said aloud. "I will show her and my stepmother and my brother and my sisters that

I, Martina Patterson, born and raised in the ghetto will go to university and do my best, so help me God. I, Martina Patterson will leave the back of this house one day and find a place for myself and my family, even if it happens when I am old and bent."

She sneered at her reflection in the mirror and then looked at it defiantly, daring it to challenge her.

Two

It was almost two-o-clock and Martina's father had not called or come to the house. She did her chores while looking out anxiously for him. The day before, the warm summer sun had heaped its venom on helpless nature, extracting the last bit of moisture from the thirsty plants. Like a bully, it had pummelled them until they hung flaccid and forlorn, helplessly hoping for a few reviving drops of rain, but the heavens in collusion with the sun did not heed their silent cry.

When she awoke, she noticed that the sun had not poked its playful rays through the chintz curtains and cast patterns on the wall, but it had given way to a surly sky, laden with dark grey clouds, converging in groups as though they were having a conference of conspiracy to decide whether or not to unwillingly dump water on the hopeful land. The drought had grasped the land firmly for months, making fissures in the earth which resembled overbaked pastry. The trees and plants at Aunt Indra's house were still green and cheerful because of the daily watering. There were a number of hoses and sprinklers and Martina and Yvette spent hours each week watering the plants. Martina did not mind this task because she loved being around water as she was a swimmer hoping one day to represent her country. She had scaled down a bit on this activity because she wanted her grades to be good and the many chores at home had forced her to do more studying at school, but she planned to resume with fervour when she started attending university.

Martina took up the book, 'No Stone Unturned' and got ready to read, but first decided to turn on the radio. There had to be some special weather condition which had cast such an unfriendly brooding look on the face of the sky. It was two minutes to two when the radio host commented on the weather, a tropical wave had been born and it was threatening to become a tropical depression and so the country would be experiencing rain. She ignored the negative implications and thanked God for the impending rain.

The news headlines came after the weather report and the first item caught Martina's attention.

Breaking news! There is trouble brewing at AIEXIM. Sources have told our media corporation that auditors have uncovered a staggering seventy-five-million-dollar fraud! The police have been called in and are presently questioning all the top officials of this reputable export-import company which has been in operation for over eighty years. There will be more details in subsequent newscasts. An item of news has just reached us that...

Martina sank down in the chair forgetting her book. AIEXIM was the company for which her father worked and he was not just a worker, but one of the managers. This meant that he was one of those who were being questioned! She now understood why he had not called or come to see her as he had promised. She picked up her cell phone and dialled his number several times but it went to voicemail each time. She also called his home landline hoping that he would somehow be there but there was no answer. She had known her father for only two years and knew nothing about his work or business dealings. She did not know anyone who knew him outside of his family and even if she did, she would not want to discuss her father with anyone. As far as they were concerned, especially her stepmother and sister, she was an unfortunate accident who had unceremoniously entered their lives at the death of her mother. She was no more than an item of misfortune that had surfaced to cause friction in the Patterson's household. Martina had been to their mansion on the hill only once and she knew her stepmother and siblings had spoken to her only because of her father's presence. It did not make things any better that Martina had done and was doing better at school than her siblings. She had seen the forced smiles that did not reach the eyes which they had given when her academic success had been mentioned in their presence. She had refused to go back to her father's house and he told her that he understood.

14

She did not want to share the news with Miss Fuller or Yvette because she did not know if he was involved or would turn up and laugh the whole problem away, shaking his head reassuringly and telling her not to pay attention to what negative people thought as he had done on more than one occasion when she seemed down.

Martina listened to the news headlines at four and the story remained the same, but the newscaster promised further details in the five o'clock news. Martina felt a low, hollow, undefined feeling starting up at the pit of her stomach. It rose swiftly like just added coconut milk in a covered pot and then engulfed her whole being, setting off a pulsating headache concentrated mainly at the back of her head. And then the rain came, proclaiming its presence with loud rhythmic beats on the roof and a screeching wind. Martina jumped up to close the window just as Yvette rushed in excitedly.

"Tina gal, you really pass boring! You need to come outside and see the wind and rain. It jus' different!" She held Martina's hand and pulled her to the back verandah washroom behind the two rooms. "Tina jus' look at how the rain carrying on!"

It was indeed carrying on; the trees and plants were dancing gleefully as the torrents battered them, flinging them one way, and then raising them up only to dash them mercilessly to the other side. It was like a brawny bully tormenting vulnerable victims. The rain pounded the earth, forcing it to take great gulps and then when it could take no more, the earth spat it out. As it accumulated, it coursed in rivulets at first and then steady streams which covered the grassy areas and then raced playfully around the sides of the house and then galloped down the driveway and finally merged with other bodies of water on their way to the culvert.

Martina watched it all, exulting in the intricacies of nature, grateful for the rain and wishing it could help to wash her mind of the burgeoning worry evident in the headache tugging at the back of her head. "I want to lie down a bit," she told the two who were so engrossed in the antics of the rain.

"Yes Tina go lie down and read, that's all yuh love," Yvette said, laughing at her moving back. Martina smiled to herself. She was glad that with time Yvette was returning slowly to her former talkative, teasing self. The trauma of incest which had burnt indelible scars in her life was fading a little. She did not get very good grades in her primary school exit exam but Martina's father had helped to get her into a traditional high school. She was supposed to be going into grade nine after summer and Martina and Miss Turner spent a little time each day helping her with her reading and mathematics.

Martina tried to read and sleep, but the latter was elusive and she lacked the focus for the former. She tuned in to the five o'clock news and the leading item was about her father's company.

There has been a development in the breaking news first carried by this station at two o'clock. Auditors have discovered that a whopping seventy-five million dollars have been siphoned from the company AIEXIM over a period of ten years. The police were early on the scene and tried to carry out top level investigations but only two of the four managers could be found. The other two, whose names have been withheld, could not be traced up to news time. The police suspect that they have either left the island or have gone into hiding. As a result, all their assets have been frozen and the police have stepped up surveillance at their homes, both international airports, and other ports of exit.

Martina turned off the radio as soon as the item was finished. She did not know whether to tell Yvette and Miss Turner about what was happening. She thought that they would find out by seven because Miss Turner always watched the seven o'clock television news and there was no way that this item would not make the news. She thought of Aunt Indra who did not always watch the news, but somewhere, somehow, somebody was bound to call her and report the news. For a reason unknown, Martina decided she would not be the harbinger. She would let her find out herself and address the matter. She called her father again but to no avail, only silence reigned supreme.

During the seven o'clock news, Yvette burst into the room

with Miss Turner in tow. "Tina! Tina!" She was breathless as if she had been running for miles. Her eyes were large with surprise and excitement. "Tina, yuh hear the news about your father? Yuh mus' have! Tina yuh need to call him an' fine out what they really talking about! A sure him not involved in anything bad!"

"Yvette calm down, calm down," Miss Turner begged, seating herself on the bed close to Martina. The lines on her face were contracting and expanding, expressing the emotions which her voice was trying to hide. "Tina a feel yuh hear about this before now. Yuh did seem a little uptight an' silent today. Why yuh never say anything to me? Yuh call yuh father? What him say him going on?" For Miss Turner who always spoke in a halting manner as if words hurt her tongue, the words came out fast, bumping into and tumbling over one another.

Martina had tried to prepare herself for the onslaught of questions but now she found it difficult to answer. The shivery feeling which had been born earlier was now a part of her. "Yes I heard it on the news but never want to say anything because the details were too sketchy but now they seem to know more." She held her head down as she spoke, trying to keep them from seeing the climbing fear in her eyes. "And yes a call my father several times but silence is the only answer I got. Just silence..." Her voice petered off having a similar silence as the one she had got from her father.

"A jus' hope him not involved cause I don't know what would happen to us," Yvette blurted out loudly, voicing the concern that was on everybody's mind. She always had a way of speaking without really thinking, impetuous they called it.

"Everything will turn out right," Martina said, but the optimism did not reach her voice, it somehow seemed stuck in her throat.

"Well we have to wait an' see, an' advice to all of us is not to start the worrying before we really know what we are worrying about. Don't let we cross the bridge before it even go up good," Miss Turner admonished.

Martina always saw Miss Turner as a fountain of practicality. She always thought she was aptly named as she always gave good advice and was a catalyst for important turning points and not one given to will-o-the wisps ideas.

Long after everyone had gone to bed, Martina lay thinking about the implications of her father being in trouble, the thoughts just rained ceaselessly like the constant crash of waves in a rough sea during a storm. How would they manage? Where would she get the money to go to university? What would people think? The foray of questions continued like the relentless tide and there was an ebb only when sleep overpowered her and calmed the waves in her mind.

She woke up suddenly and jack-knifed into a sitting position. For the moment, she felt disoriented and willed her mind to focus. Yvette was sleeping across from her, her body almost at the edge of the bed. The sheet was rumpled and exposed the mattress at the foot of the bed. I was not the only one that had a rough night ride, Martina thought.

She hurried out of bed, grabbed her cell phone and made for the bathroom. She did not want to wake Yvette while she listened to the radio.

It was not quite six o'clock so while she was waiting for the news, she called her father. As it had been the previous day, there was no answer, save for the rehearsed, irritating voice from the voice mail. She turned to the news and almost fell into the bath – she was sitting on the edge – when the first item hit her.

To continue the breaking news on the AIEXIM saga, the police have reported that two of the company's four managers were shot and killed in two separate incidents last night. The first one was shot as he drove through his automated garage gate and the other was shot as he was leaving the company after a lengthy meeting with other officials. The police have refused to release their names until their families have been notified.

The phone fell with a clatter from Martina's hand as the item ended. Her mouth gaped like a fish on dry land gasping for air as she sat in shocked silence, ignoring the agitated voice of Miss Turner who was shouting for her from the room.

She walked out to her in a daze like a tight rope walker or a clown on stilts. Yvette was now awake. She sat in the bed, rubbing her eyes.

"Why can't people sleep in their bed in peace during holiday time? What you all shouting an' carrying on about so early in the morning?" She stopped rubbing her eyes and looked from Miss Turner to Martina and the look she saw on their faces knocked the sleep out of her eyes and sent her over to Martina. She grabbed her sister around the waist and asked in a small, scared voice, "Tina is Mr. Patterson okay? Is he? You hear from him? Tell me quick!" By now she was shaking her, fright pulping from her eyes.

Martina put her arms around her sister reassuringly. "No Yvette, not yet. A mean a don't hear from him yet, but there is more trouble because they have killed two of the other managers." She stopped, the words stuck in her throat; she did not want to express her fears. A little vestige of hope was still left trying to surge forward through the despair that was dampening everything else.

"Eeeeh." Yvette made a sound like a frightened baby mouse caught in a trap. She grasped Martina as if she were a life belt and buried her face in her nightie.

Bang! Bang! Bang! There were impatient sounds coming from outside the room. They could only be coming from one person because Aunt Indra lived alone and except for when the helper was around or her three children visited, no one else came into the house.

The three looked at one another, not certain what Aunt Indra's reaction would be like. She always seemed to love her nephew but forgot that Martina was also her grandniece in her attitude towards her. Miss Turner hurried to open the door and Martina and Yvette stood where they were. She was leaning on the door and when Miss Turner opened it, she fell forward grasping the lock as a parasite clinging fiercely to a tree for sustenance.

Yvette choked back a laugh and despite the seriousness of the situation, a faint smile surfaced around the corners of Martina's mouth but she quickly supressed it.

"Are you stupid or what?" Aunt Indra roared at Miss Turner. "Didn't you hear me knocking the door and must have seen the lock moving? You people from the lower class don't seem to have much sense!"

"And people from the upper class knowing that ghetto people fool fool should try to protect themselves from the fools. That mean you should neva lean on the door." She leered at her and almost laughed at the comical picture of the glasses askew on Aunt Indra's face. She had not bothered to fix them but was staring through one while her nose peeped through the other.

Martina gave Miss Turner the 'don't continue to argue with her look' and Miss Turner walked over to where Martina was standing and faced Aunt Indra.

She fixed the glasses and then looked at them in a supercilious manner. "I guess you must have heard the news." Without waiting for affirmation she continued, "Have you heard from your father since he came here the other day?"

"No," said Martina, her throat had become cracked and painful like when she had influenza. The act of talking was sending fingers of pain poking in her throat. "I have been calling him for two days now but he has not answered." Her voice petered off into painful nothingness.

"Well, I certainly hope that the two men who the police…"

Aunt Indra stopped talking.

For the first time Martina noticed that she was genuinely concerned and shaken. She apparently thought highly of her nephew but not of his bastard daughter and her appendages. Martina tried to understand the situation; her father's family members were all accustomed to her stepmother and the children. Suddenly, out of nowhere this child born of indiscretion had surfaced into their life, more academically inclined than the legitimate ones and invoking pity because her mother was dead and heaven would have further frowned on the father if he had not assumed some form of financial responsibility for a child he had neglected for years. Well, Martina thought, none of this is my fault. I did not commit this Class A felony, my parents did. Why do I have to suffer for it?

"We just have to listen out to hear who is dead." Aunt Indra managed to say the hated word. "I suppose that since his family is away you would be the one they would contact if anything. I hope he is not one of those two men…" Her emotional demeanour was obvious; she was fearful, almost distraught and on the fringe of hysteria. She left abruptly without looking back.

Despite her usual aura, Martina felt sorry for her. She hoped none of them would have to face the ultimate. When she was gone, everyone just sat on Martina's bed in solemn silence, waiting, waiting, waiting.

In about five minutes the door was wrenched open. They all jumped in fright as Aunt Indra appeared again. She stood in the doorway and announced, "The police called and they are coming to see you." She looked at Martina, her face reflecting their fright.

"Did they say why?" Martina managed feebly. "Did they say why?" she repeated foolishly, hoping and not hoping for an answer.

Aunt Indra shook her head, unable to speak. Dried tear tracks were visible on her face. No sooner had she left the room than a siren was heard wailing in earnest. Martina stayed where she was, transfixed to the spot; if she had been standing in front of a moving vehicle heading directly for her, she would have been hit. She knew that Aunt Indra was going to open the electronic gate. She knew that the police were going to drive through the gate. She knew they would wail their way up the driveway. She knew they would get out of the car. She knew they would come to her and she knew she might faint or scream.

Yvette and Miss Turner came into the room and held her hands on either side, still she did not move. She was a tree anchored by fear and watered by problems; her roots of trials and tribulation just kept on growing, spreading her sadness and daunting her progress. Her leaves which were her achievements were drooping under the onslaught of disappointment and death.

She knew that Aunt Indra came into the room and called her name but she did not answer. She felt herself being propelled by hands, Yvette and Miss Turner's. They pushed her into the living room and she saw the policemen, solemn and sombre eyes digging into her like forks in the earth. She could not feel her feet, they were frozen into thin sticks of ice and her palms were melting. She heard the police officer's voice from a distance; she read his lips rather than heard his abrasive voice.

"When last have you seen your father?"

"Seen who? Seen my father?" Fear and confusion had become allies.

"Young lady, we have no time to fool around! What are you hiding?" The older of the two police officers advanced towards her. He was almost touching her and Martina's mind which was thawing, registered his black bean eyes and his twitching moustache. For some reason he reminded Martina of a tarantula, maybe because his moustache was very thick and kept moving. A thin elbow scar enclosed his left eye.

"Hiding who or what?" Martina responded staring back at the police officer. "What are you talking about?"

"Don't pretend innocence girl, a talking about your father. Is he hiding here?" the younger of the two officers bellowed at Martina. Unlike the first officer, his face was smooth and clean-shaven with steady, searching black eyes. His nostrils flared at short intervals, expressing his impatience at Martina's seemingly evasive responses.

"So he isn't dead then." The enormity of her relief spread across her face, and brought her eyes to life and relaxed her features somewhat.

"No he is not dead, not that we know of, but we need him

like yesterday, dead or alive!" the senior officer said.

"When last did you see or hear from him?" Bean Eyes asked.

"Two days ago, he came here to see me. I have been calling him since but no response."

"Well we will soon know if he is here. Search the place!" he yelled, looking over his shoulder. Three more officers appeared.

"Wait, where is your warrant?" Aunt Indra enquired. "You can't just come barging in here without proper permission."

The senior officer waived a sheet of paper in Aunt Indra's face and then followed the men while the whole household followed them.

"I hear too many times that you people plant things in people's house and then send them to prison," Aunt Indra remarked. "So I am sticking to you like burr."

"Stick all you want to. We are doing our search," the senior officer said, "and what you just said is not true about the police. Where did you get such erroneous information?" He glared at her fiercely but Aunt Indra equalled his stare.

"Fisherman never yet say his fish stink so why should I believe anything you say? Just don't break or damage anything inside my house because you did not buy anything inside here!" Aunt Indra warned the officer, pushing out her mouth like a pig's snout.

He dismissed her with a wave of his hand and joined the others in peering in and around closets and cupboards, and looking under beds and tables. They searched everywhere with the quartet trailing them like liquid from a broken container. After they had satisfied themselves that Mr. Patterson was not around, they left but not without warning everyone that criminal charges could be made against them for harbouring a criminal. When Martina asked them what were the charges against her father, the senior officer said, "Suspicion of stealing millions of dollars from company funds."

After they left there was silence for a while, each person was submerged in thought:

Aunt Indra: What is this in my old age? If I had not let this ghetto no place girl in this house this would not have happened!

Miss Turner: What a thing, a wonder what this going to mean for us especially Tina, my God!

Yvette: Please God let dem fine him so dat he can still help us. Please God.

Martina: Lord, I don't like this; is my father hurt somewhere? Has he gone away? Is he really guilty?

Aunt Indra interrupted the train of thoughts. "This is not going to work. I do not want any more police in this house that my dead husband and I worked so hard to buy. As long as you are here girl, they are going to keep coming here and I will not stand for it!" She pounded her right fist into her left palm and winced when the stones on her wedding ring made contact with her flesh.

"But Aunt Indra, I don't think they came here just

because of me, remember you are my father's aunt. You are related to him as well. If he has done something wrong the shame is not just on me but on the whole family!" Martina emphasized the 'whole family'.

"Yes, but you are closer, you are Martin's daughter." She glared at Martina, daring her to argue otherwise while wishing this was not so.

"You know Aunt Indra, since this problem started it is even clearer that you only try to be nice when my father is around. You only tolerate us because of the money he usually give to you." She watched her aunt's face to see her reaction but her features remained constant, betraying none of what was happening inside.

"Guess what? You are so right. Who you think want a bunch of ghetto people pack up in them house? Even with your pretty talking you don't belong here! Up here so is not for you and this is the right time for you to leave this place and return to your roots!" She looked from one to the other, regarding them like stray dogs who had pushed their way under her fence and were eating the food thrown out in her backyard.

Everyone saw the look and heard the words and cringed. So it was finally out, Martina thought. She had been right all along. They were not wanted there in that upper class neighbourhood.

"What you mean back to where we come from?" Yvette asked in a small frightened voice.

"You're not so bright but you know exactly what I mean.

Let me spell it out, I want you to leave my house and go back to where you came from, Dinsland, Dumpland whatever it name. You think I am going to find money to feed you and pay bills for you so you can exalt yourself? I'm tired of explaining to my friends and everyone else what you doing in my house. Now I can stop the pretence." Her words kept pounding and digging into her listeners, making deep wedges and holes.

"But we don't have anywhere to go back to and what if Tina father turn up?" Yvette said lamely; her alarm effacing the hurt feelings. "What is so different about us?" she further asked, trying to unearth the arcana of class relations.

"You are certainly different. Some people were born in a certain place, they talk funny and everything about them is just weird, they just don't belong and so are you. You are like school in the summer, no class. You can take the pig to any environment you want but the grunt will still be in it!" Aunt Indra was certainly heated up; the volcano had erupted and was spewing out molten insults.

"Well for one who was not born with a gold spoon in her mouth and had to work hard to get all this, you are certainly a good one to talk. Is right down a Donkey Pass in a St. James you come from. It take one nobody to know another nobody," said Miss Turner.

"But Aunt Indra why you talking like that? Since my father is not around I thought I could ask you to help me with university. At least help me get a loan and I will pay it back when I start working and I could work weekends to pay the rent and help Yvette to go to school." Desperation had crept into Martina's voice. She was clutching at the wind trying to appeal to her aunt's better nature.

"Me, help you get loan to attend university! You must be crazy! Be glad that you get away and achieve the few subjects, but as far as I am concerned that is your actualization! I will never put myself into any trouble to help any of you! By the way make certain that by next week you leave this house!" She walked away without looking back; her work had been done, the ultimatum delivered.

"But Aunt Indra…" Martina started, the pain and tears choking her.

Miss Turner grabbed the crying girl and hugged her trembling body. "Now Tina, don't bother to cry. A know how you feel but one day somehow you will realize your dreams. Leave Indra alone, time will take care of people like her."

"But Miss Turner how am I ever going to get to university with no money. The little I have saved is not much, it can't pay the tuition fee and it's too late for student's loan now." Martina felt hot tears of despondency coursing down her cheeks. She was not a person who cried much but since this whole episode with her father, the tears just seemed to have a mind of their own and fell unbidden, heedlessly, making her seem weak and spineless.

"Tina we must find a place to live, we must, even if it mean going back to Dinsland. We not going to live on the street." Despite herself, Miss Turner's voice sounded dead, hopelessness had crept in robbing it of the usual confidence and buoyancy. Martina felt when something slumped and swiftly snapped in her spirit. She was wallowing in wretchedness before even trying.

She pulled herself away from Miss Turner and immediately Yvette came and hugged her, her silence feeding the despair of the moment. Martina slowly unlocked herself from the embrace and fought to regain her equilibrium. She had to decide on the next move as living on the sidewalk was not an option.

"Miss Turner, Yvette, we have to think out this thing. Let us go outside under the trees and see if nature can offer some sort of solution." Martina fought to control the quivering in her voice. I have come through many difficulties in this life, let me not give up so easily, she inwardly chided herself. I am born to fight. I have the blood of my African ancestors in me. Emancipation was not achieved by feeble minded individuals but by plucky, resolute people who were like Moses to the Israelites and Paul Bogle in the Morant Bay Rebellion. They had not built railroads to freedom so that the downtrodden would sink in the mire of melancholy and misery; but so that the message was clear that fighting, not necessarily physically, but with wits and faith, could carry you through.

Three

They sat under a tree in the backyard to plan strategies for their survival. The atmosphere, in keeping with their spirits, was sullen and heavy. The sun had withdrawn its golden glory and the wind soughed and sighed in the trees as though mourning about something. The loaded clouds crouched closely to the earth intentionally, ready to water the land like Yvette's tears which still flowed freely down her face.

"Yvette, please stop the crying, weak hearts never win fierce battles. We have to live and live to plan. There has to be a way out of this Egypt. We have to cross the Red Sea or die in the wilderness of poverty."

Yvette looked at her a little mystified, understanding only the reference to poverty. Meanwhile Miss Turner was on her cell phone talking to someone in Dinsland.

"Yes Nerva, how yuh do, how everything down there?" She listened for a while and then she said, "Oh so a who dem a fire di shot?" Paused. "Cobra Yutes, yuh mean the teenage gang dat form since we leave down there?" She listened, opening her eyes wide in disbelief. "Say what, shooting every night an' t'ree people dead since month! A wah di hell yuh a tell mi seh?" She listened again then exclaimed, "Where, in my house an' Miss Fuller house? So what happen to di people dem dat live there before dem?" She listened intently again before responding, "A lie yuh telling, run dem out an' tek over! So why yuh never call me an' tell me before now?" She listened again and then said, "Aright, yuh know the credit story, mi wi call yuh again." She hung up and just sat looking at the dark, disagreeable clouds breaking away from one another. That was exactly what was happening to Martina's family she thought; the erosion of family support and care, the disintegration of forged relationships built over the past two years had been dealt a blow by unforeseen circumstances.

"So we can't go back to Dinsland," Yvette commented, her voice held both relief and sadness. Relief, because it would be a retrograde step to go back to the negative side of where you were coming from, and sadness because where else could they go if there was no money to pay rent?

"Listen to this plan," Martina said, bringing them back together. "I have a little money saved from my lunch money and so on. If we can find a big room somewhere we can live together and if I don't get to go to university a can find a job so that Yvette can go to school and when a save enough a can go to university and get my degree."

"That sound good," said Yvette, "But what if you don't

get any job?"

"Don't start thinking negatively, we just have to try. Nothing tried, nothing done. A can still study and get a little job on campus, but because it is so late now and I don't have any contacts it will be kind of difficult and I need to keep an eye on you," Martina said to Yvette.

"An eye on me, but why? I can take care of myself, I am a big girl now." Yvette pouted her disagreement.

"Dat is exactly why yuh need someone to take care a yuh because yuh is a big girl," Miss Turner pointed out. "A not so young anymore an' yuh mother not around so Tina an' me responsible for yuh whether yuh like it or not, we have to see that yuh go right." Miss Turner's voice was serious, conveying her concern and forcibly bringing back to them the ordeal Yvette had been through and was still trying to recover from; physical and mental scars normally took years to heal.

"You behaving as if I am a bad girl that everybody need to watch." Yvette was not enjoying being the centre of attention.

Miss Turner changed the path of the conversation. "Tina a was t'inking what about yuh friends, Leonie an' Andre, yuh t'ink they could help yuh out, maybe ask their mother to stand security for yuh to get the money to study?"

"Miss Turner you know that you are really a good thinker, I called both of them last night and Leonie said her mother was already a guarantor for somebody and Andre and his family are somewhere out of the country and a not getting through to them, so that is dead. I really don't know any of my father's family that well to ask for help, so again, dead end."

It was Shimron, Martina's brother, who lived in one of the inner city communities below Cross Roads that actually found a place for Martina in the same yard that he lived. A family had just moved out of two bedrooms with a small bathroom and a tiny kitchen and he impressed upon the landlord to give it to his 'friends'.

A week later they left Aunt Indra's house. It was very early in the morning as Martina did not want the whole world to witness their descent. It was a godsend that her father had bought a few pieces of furniture and appliances for them rather than let them use everything that belonged to his aunt. She had two double beds, two armchairs, a dresser, a chest of drawers, a television, a refrigerator and a stove as well as other small items.

Aunt Indra stood by as the workmen loaded the furniture on the small moving truck which had cut a huge slice out of Martina and Miss Turner's finances. To everyone's humiliation, she had visibly searched everything that came out of her house. The workmen looked at the three females as if they were thieves. Yvette started to cry but Martina and Miss Turner kept their composure. As they climbed into the vehicle, Miss Turner turned and looked at Aunt Indra, raw bitterness flowing from her eyes.

"If a don't die before yuh, a will read or hear bout how God deal with yuh case. A encourage yuh to seek him!"

Aunt Indra stood stock still, her repartee frozen on her slightly opened lips. Maybe she was reliving the evil comments she had hurled at Martina and Yvette the previous night. While they were packing, she had gone into Martina's room unannounced.

"Why are you making so much noise in the house?" she demanded gruffly, her belly pushing forward in a menacing manner.

"Sorry Aunt Indra, we are just packing up our things. Sorry for the noise," Martina apologized.

"Packing up things, if Martin never fool-fool and use him good good money buy them few things you would never have anything to pack up. You would go just like you came, poor beggars from the ghetto!" She lowered her eyes and widened her lips as if she were smelling filth.

"Yes we are poor with dignity, where's the crime?" Martina had fired back, tired of the constant belittling of their status.

"Poor with dignity indeed! If Martin never rescued you when he did, you would be standing at the street corner selling your scrawny body just like you are going to do to get into university, scum of society!"

She had started walking away but was stopped in her tracks as Yvette grabbed her in the back. Martina had not seen her move until she grabbed her. Both she and Miss Turner had jumped forward as the woman cried out, and pried Yvette away. She was breathing heavily like she was going into cardiac arrest and was crying, but hastily escaped like an animal fleeing a trap. Martina felt she realized that she had provoked the attack.

Now she just stood and stared at Miss Turner and as the truck rattled noisily away, the frozen look became a sinister sneer.

They arrived at Port-Herb Street, an inner city area downtown, close to the sea. The buildings at the entrance were assorted, some of them were one and two-room huts made from zinc and ply board and some even boasted glass windows. The other houses were concrete structures in an advanced state of dilapidation, the walls were so blanched you could not tell the true colours which had been sucked out by the continual fury of the fuming sun and the constant battering of the rain. Those that were extremely close to the sea also suffered from the unrelenting, unending ebbing of the tide.

The buildings that were further down the street were in a better condition; apparently it was the original housing scheme. The houses were two bedrooms with a single small bathroom and a kitchen at the back. Some people had made additions to the existing structures but the space was so limited that the wall ended up being a shared one between the neighbouring houses. These houses that had been added to became a two-family house or one half was used for business enterprises of all descriptions – restaurants, hairdressing parlours, betting shops, wholesales, ordinary grocery shops, dancehalls, night clubs, marketing outlets, just name it, you had it. Shimron's home was close to an empty lot where a garage and a market of sorts were neighbours.

Potholes of various sizes and shapes which defied description, dotted the street. Some of them had smelly green-black water as their permanent resident. Sparse green plants and a few fruit trees struggled for survival as the mass of concrete forced them to cower and fight for standing room.

Even though the morning was young, people were already up and about. It was a Saturday and business started early and ended late. Stray dogs and cats roved leisurely, sniffing, scratching, climbing and barking and mewing in short snaps.

As they alighted from the vehicle, a number of onlookers gathered a few yards away. They whispered and pointed, one of them even walked up to the pick-up and touched a piece of the furniture. Martina winced as if she were the one being touched. Already she was assaulted by the piquant smell of ganja and because of her allergy to smoke, already her migraine was intensifying. At this point, Shimron came out accompanied by his girlfriend who was holding a young baby. Martina had not seen her brother since the last six months when he had visited her at school. He had not liked going to Aunt Indra's house because he said as he reached the gate the inhospitable atmosphere greeted him. He had told the trio the very first time he visited that it was only because of Mr. Patterson why that woman had allowed them to pass through her gate. She had not fooled him.

As Martina looked at Shimron, she marvelled at the great transformation he had made since their mother's death. Despite his involvement in the drug trade a benevolent police officer had helped him to find a new lease on life. He had learnt the skills of masonry and upholstery, and when jobs could be had he managed to make a living. She looked at him with warmth forming in her heart which momentarily snuffed out the coldness which had clamped her heart. He had grown to almost six-feet and had put on a considerable amount of weight. Even though his face had become more relaxed, it had grown more angular and serious. His eyes, though not unfriendly, had a steady unwavering gaze which suggested he meant business. He wore his hair in long cornrows and his passion for earrings was still real. Martina could not help but notice his biceps, the lifting and constant use of his arms had strengthened his muscles; they reminded her of two intertwined chain links.

She did not know his child's mother. She seemed too young and should be in school, Martina thought. The story was the same as always, many teenage girls in the inner city became mothers too quickly, robbing themselves of much of their own childhood. This girl did not appear to be more than fifteen years old. She was short and of slight built with huge staring eyes like those set in a doll's face, they seemed deeply fixed and unblinking. There was something false about them and Martina soon realized she wore long false eye lashes which were in sync with the black false horse-mane hair which flowed around her shoulders. The baby seemed too big for her to hold properly.

"Hi Tina, hi Yvette, hi Miss T," Shimron greeted them. "Glad to see you again."

The gaiety in his voice did not reach his eyes. He would have preferred to be the only one fighting it out in the inner city and even though they had not been one hundred percent happy in their bourgeois setting, he would have preferred that they had remained there. There were too many dangers in the inner city and he thought the girls had already had their share of life-jerking escapades. Now, he was a man and he was expecting anything to happen to him at any time but he would not go looking for it. He was finished with drugs and breaking the law.

"This is my girlfriend Nadra and as you can see you are an aunt." He proudly took his son from Nadra and held him out to the three for approval. They all shook his hand and tickled him. They could see their mother in his convulsed toothless smile.

He handed his son back to Nadra and then went to help the trio arrange the furniture and get settled in. The walls had been hurriedly painted, the uneven brush marks stared through the blue one-coat paint. They felt the heat pouring in and no wonder because it was a slab roof, the wall was low and the rooms were small, almost as small as the ones they had lived in, in Dinsland. The only difference was that they did not have to share the bathroom with everyone in close proximity, and what a bathroom! It was no more than four and a half square feet with a shower, a toilet bowl of undetermined colour and a heavily scarred basin.

As soon as Shimron left, Yvette lay down on the bed she would share with Martina and started to cry. Martina was expecting some kind of rain because Yvette had been quietly scowling for two days, but the torrent that came with howling and Yvette kicking about like an object being thrashed by the wind was pathetic.

Martina rushed to her and tried to hug her but she did not succeed. She tried reasoning with her instead. "Yvette you know the reason we had to come to this place." She tried to be calm and gentle. The only response was accelerated sobbing, vroom, vroom like a truck changing gears to go over Spur Tree Hill.

"Yvette, listen to me, you know me more than anyone else would never come to live in these kind a place again." She allowed the words to register before she went on. "You know I would have chosen somewhere better but if we did, we would have to move in a month or two because we cannot pay the rent. A have to choose somewhere that we can manage the rent and still send you to school. You must finish school because education is a way out of poverty especially when you black and low class and come from the inner city. It's a way out from getting pregnant every year for a different man who does not want anything but to play with you until you get pregnant and then disappear. Look at what happened to mummy! All three of us are for three different fathers! Education can help to lift our standard and make us appreciate ourselves as women and black people. I'm going to start hunting for a job by Monday and if I get a steady one in a few months we will move out of this place. Like you, a really don't want to be here but I'm grinning and bearing it until I can see my way out. In the meantime, we have to keep ourselves to ourselves, walk on a chalk line and keep ourselves out of mix-up. Yvette girl we have to make it out of here!" She lay down beside her and tried to hug her but even though she had quietened considerably, she turned her back and refused to talk.

"Yvette, all dat Tina just say is gospel." Miss Turner had come into the room and stood listening while Martina was talking but did not wish to interrupt her. She was proud of Martina and her maturity in handling their present challenges. "Yvette, a know how you feel, a feel the same way too but we can't do anything until Mr. Patterson business straighten out. He is the one that did help us. Tina really trying her best but yuh know she don't have the money. We have to stay on crooked until we can cut straight; we have to endure the hardships until better come. Just hold up yuh head like Tina an' try hard an' God will help us. Jus' don't get mix up with the crowd." She sat on the bed and stared fixedly at the wall as if it could offer support. She did not love giving long speeches but when they were needed she rose to the occasion. Even before the children's mother had died she had somehow felt responsible for them and now more than ever back in the inner city, she felt responsibility pressing down on her like a bag of stones and her age was becoming a problem. Her body was riddled with arthritis and her blood pressure had a mind of its own, sometimes leaping almost out of bounds, not to mention her sinuses which became inflamed easily, triggered off by excessive dust, spicy seasoning etc. Still she was holding on as best as she could; she felt she had to, for the children's sake.

Yvette spent the rest of the afternoon in bed, sometimes watching television, sometimes staring at the wall seeing what no one else could see. She refused to eat or even look through the window and often hugged herself and rocked to and fro.

Four

It was eight o'clock, the following Monday morning when Martina left the house with Shimron. She did not feel comfortable walking out by herself in this strange place, so he had decided to walk with her to the bus stop on his way to work. Miss Turner was the only one who had left the house since they had moved in. She had heard about a church down the road and had gone to it.

Even at eight in the morning the street was alive with people and Martina wondered aloud if that street ever went to sleep for long.

"Shimron, are there always people on this street?" Martina's voice reflected her surprise.

"My girl, there is always some kind of activity going on here. Member that this is a seaside place an' all kind of illegal activity taking place here, but when gunshot start buss only the criminal dem on the street. Right now nothin' much going on but nobody should feel comfortable. But don't worry, a know you not the mix-up type and I learn my lesson so nobody should come looking for us, cool." Shimron tried to keep his voice steady and low but Martina had grown up in the inner city and she was cognizant of much that took place in these kinds of communities.

Martina did not want to work in the downtown area so she went to some places out of the inner city. At each she left a resume and one personnel manager called her back when she was leaving and spoke to her.

"Your subjects are mainly arts oriented and your grades are excellent. Why aren't you in a university or planning to go to one?"

"My father does not have the money right now, so I have to work for a while," Martina answered, hoping she would not continue to question her about her father.

"But what kind of work does he do and why didn't you apply for students' loan?" the personnel officer insisted.

"He works seasonally doing all kinds of things from mason work to carpentry and I didn't think about the loan until it was too late." Her riposte was unrehearsed but sounded convincing.

"This address that you have on this resume, where is this place?" She looked Martina straight in the eyes as if she did not expect a veracious reply.

"It is downtown right by the seaside." Her answer was frank, without hesitation.

"Okay, I have an idea where it is. Alright I will get back to you."

Martina had a sinking feeling as she knew that her

address was a problem. She had been naïve enough to think that her grades would overshadow it. What were these people looking for, good grades and a decent hardworking person or someone whose address defined him or her? She had been warned about these types of people before.

The message became even clearer when she was called for an interview a week later. Five minutes into the interview, the interviewer, a gentleman whose hairline was obviously in malice with his forehead, so far had it distanced itself from his youthful face and whose ears in alliance with his hairline stood aloof from his face, asked her the dreaded question.

"How did someone like you manage to make it to such an exclusive school and attain these excellent passes?"

The question was out and Martina's keen eyes detected a slight movement as the fellow interviewer kicked the man's foot.

"What do you mean someone like me" Martina questioned. She abhorred the insinuation, 'someone like you'. She must really be a societal upstart trying to usurp her position in an Indian caste system!

The man must have seen the offended look on her face and smarting from the kick, he tried to downplay his embarrassment. "I don't mean it that way. I mean, I'm not saying you are not bright and that bright people can't come from these type of areas as indicated by your address, but it is strange that you ended up at Milverton. That is top of the line." He was fighting hard to choose the right words. Slight sweat broke out on his extended forehead and he started twiddling his fingers.

Martina took advantage of his discomfiture, she was not an alien to elitism and knew just how to answer. "Well sir, truth is sometimes stranger than fiction, but if many of the inner city youths were given a chance they would have done better academically and if those who somehow outdo the odds were given credit for it and treated like the ordinary humans they are instead of trying to earn a degree in trying to prove their self-worth, we would have a better world. Thank you for allowing someone like me to enter your upper-class establishment." With that she dismissed herself.

As she walked towards the door, she could not pretend not to hear the fiery fumes which had been sparked by the exchange.

"Mr. Hylton that was totally uncalled for! You literally insulted the young lady. You need to be more tactful with how you treat people, especially those who are intelligent. I suppose when I tell you where I am coming from you are going to have me fired because my life was much less than humble!"

The rest of the conversation was lost as Martina walked away thinking that old injuries and demons were somehow related in that they never went away.

She did not want to tell Miss Turner everything but when she did not have any good news to give her, she told her about the classism, elitism and the supercilious attitude of her interviewers. She observed that it was sad to know that in the twenty-first century, more than a century and a half after emancipation, in a predominantly black country with many people in the upper echelon of society who had risen from the gutter of poverty to their exalted positions, inner city people were still branded like slaves or cattle and some were still being placed on the auction blocks as human trafficking was rife.

"But Tina, yuh young but yuh go through enough to know that in some instance we are right back where we coming from. The more things change is the more they remain the same. Our heroes, especially those who fight for poor people don't get no time to rest in their grave cause they keep on turning every minute, every minute when the injustice tek place." Miss Turner had an accusatory look in her eyes, the pleats of wrinkles in her face were drawn together even closer. The cruel prangs of discrimination and deprivation made ever deeper furrows in her heart, as over the years she had hoped that with the rapid promulgation of knowledge and technology the disease would have been stemmed, not spreading like a mosquito borne disease.

Martina became hopeful of getting a job in one instance when she was shortlisted and called to do a second interview for a huge corporation. She was encouraged because the usual discriminatory questions had been missing from the first interview.

When the interview was almost finished one lady of the panel of three directed a question at Martina.

"I notice that your name is Martina Patterson, are you in any way related to Martin Patterson? Something about your name sets off a bell clanging in my head." Her sharp gaze tried to pierce Martina's exterior.

"Martin Patterson! Which Martin Patterson?" Martina was taken off guard, she had not expected this line of questioning. She had to search swiftly for an answer.

"Do you listen to the news at all? There is the scandal and murders associated with AIEXIM Corporation and one of the missing executives is Martin Patterson who is suspected of being involved in the grand theft." She peered at Martina again as if she were near-sighted and could not see her properly.

"Well Miss, if you do a check you will find out that there are a number of persons with this surname and it doesn't mean they are related at all." Martina was being evasive. She would not tell this woman the truth. Her mother had not given her the correct birth certificate at first but at her death she had given her the correct one and her father had gone through different legal channels to change her surname and her school records to Patterson. This had made Martina proud and filled with self-worth; a sense of belonging had washed over her like the warm glow from a welcome light on a cold night.

She knew that humans had the tendency to visit the parents' sins on their children, even the unborn generation; to put it bluntly, the interviewer's tone and question were implying that if Martin Patterson the thief was her father, then their company did not need the daughter of a thief to come and steal from them.

"No, I don't know him," said Martina, twiddling her toes and she would not have been surprised if a cock had materialized from somewhere and started crowing. She was so mortified, she hoped if her father were alive, he would never find out how she had betrayed him, especially after he had gone through so much to give her his name. To cement the fact that she didn't know any Martin Patterson, she posited a question. "If I were Martin Patterson's relation why would I be here looking for a job? I would have some of those millions to help me." She felt as if her missile had struck but another of the interviewer's question blocked it.

"Why not, as far as we have heard all his financial assets have been frozen and the police are keeping their eyes on his other possessions, so if you are related to him he wouldn't be able to help you at all."

Her words hit Martina hard as if she had walked blindfolded into a stone wall but she stared back at the lady boldly, hiding the smarting mental pain. She changed the focus of her questions and at the end Martina knew she would not get that all important call. Well, she decided, since I am not good enough to work away from the inner city I won't be a plague anymore. I will look for a job within my class, maybe I have been an upstart and uppity, let me get back to my level. She started walking around downtown seeking a job, but even the lowly had no jobs for her, there was either no vacancy or she was too qualified. One person remarked, "You must have done something wrong why you can't get a job with this kind of qualification, or maybe you have stolen somebody else papers." She looked at Martina like she was a thief who was begging for mercy. Martina really felt like hitting her and stealing away, maybe then she would know what stealing was!

While all of this was happening, Martina's precious meagre resource was dwindling. School would be opened in a few days and Yvette had not received everything she needed. She had become surly and uncommunicative and Miss Turner and Martina concluded that a taste of the high life had poured venom in her heart for anything less. Martina felt her soul sinking into her soles. It was almost as if she were experiencing going out on a boat full of holes; she had no oars and she was sinking into the enveloping abyss with little hope of being rescued. Shimron had decided to help but with a stay-at-home girlfriend, a baby and inconsistent jobs, this help would be minimal. Martina did not want to become dependent on him or anyone else, she wanted to work for Yvette, Miss Turner and herself.

In addition to being perturbed about Yvette, Martina had become anxious about her brother. She had noticed that his face had become sombre and his lips set. He was never a great talker but his words had become fewer. She wondered if the additional financial burden as regards Yvette was bothering him. She did not want to ask him or mention anything to her sister and Miss Turner.

That night she could not sleep as she was contemplating a plan of action that had surfaced out of desperation. She did not even want to discuss it with herself much less with her family. She was not sure she could go through with it, she felt she did not have the nerve, but if she could, it would be better than being dependent on anyone; a quarter of bread was better than no bread at all. As she thought about the plan, her hands and feet became moist and tremulous and her mind wavered like a tall, slim plant being swayed by the wind. She reached for a novel; reading would block the fear and indecision and provide the balm she needed to induce sleep.

As she opened the book she heard loud voices which appeared to be coming from the front of her house. The voices were angry and the conversation was punctuated by expletives, one of the hallmarks of Port-Herb; the other being the smoking of cannabis. Whenever Martina went outside or walked to the bus stop, she was always confronted by mere teenagers whose palms were a threshing floor for dry cannabis, their fingers, the equipment for grinding.

Martina crept silently to the window, not wishing to be detected, if the noise was at her door, she would never open it. From her years of living in the inner city, she knew never to open your door at nights to anyone you did not know. She placed herself at the window and listened without even cracking it.

"My yute mek up yuh mine, yuh need to mek a decision an' soon soon!" The speaker's voice was low-pitched but rose to emphasize specific words.

A voice which sounded like Shimron's responded, "Dis is the third time yuh come wid yuh badness an' a tell yuh mi mine already, no, no a million time!"

Martina could not see Shimron's face but she could

imagine the bold, irate glare trying to pierce the softly lit night.

"My yute, yuh either in or out, an' if yuh out, yuh know what yuh have to do, so try mek up yuh mine fast, yuh have exactly one week from now!" The speaker's voice tethered on a rough bark, he was so passionate about what he had come to do and he was making certain the message was well given.

"A tell yuh what, yuh better do what yuh have to do now cause next week a same answer! Do what yuh want to do now!" Shimron's voice was low and cool. Martina was certain he was not feeling cool but had somehow resigned himself to whatever he was being threatened about. She felt like rushing outside and shielding him from danger. He had been through enough and had wrestled with and wrangled free from death after he had been shot while delivering drugs. Martina hoped he had not got entangled in illegal activities again. It was so easy to succumb to illicit pursuits in the kind of setting in which they lived, especially if one was in need.

She waited until she was certain the visitor had left and then she cautiously opened her back door and walked around to Shimron's window. It was past midnight, but her ears were assaulted by loud dancehall music which she normally tried to shut out with her earphones.

Gal yuh a hat girl, look how yuh dress, look how yuh move.

Colour inna hair, mane a flop a back, eight ears ring inna yuh ears.

Ring inna navel, shorts a ride yuh bumpa.

Gal yuh deh pan fire, an' yuh a spread de fire. Gal yuh a hat girl.

Martina wondered why women had to take the brunt and battering of some dancehall artistes who had limited topics for discussion and an even more limited choice of pastimes.

There were still many activities going on, even though the street was only lit by a few street lights which were shining uneasily and cautiously as though afraid to illuminate shadowy deeds. A few people were still sitting on their verandah and small groups of boys could be seen liming around, smoking or gambling and swearing under the reluctant street lights. Martina could also hear the splash of the sea which had blended in with the general hum of the community so at times it went unnoticed. From where she was, she could see the slightly undulating silvery sheen of the sea. It was beckoning to her to come for a swim, but she resisted as she had many times before, because she was afraid of attracting unwelcome attention to herself. Still she was determined to find a way, not going to university did not mean that she had to give up on her dream of professional swimming.

She walked around to Shimron's window and knocked. There was no response from inside so she knocked harder and whispered loudly, "It's me Tina, Shim a want to talk to you."

There was an immediate response. "Tina what the hell you doing outside at dis time of the night? You mad or stupid or what? Come round the back door quick!" There was surprised, simmering anger in his voice.

Martina went around quickly and eased through the barely opened door just as Shimron exploded like a detonated bomb.

"Tina tell me what couldn't stay till mornin' to talk bout! Tell me why you have to come outside at this late time when you know how dangerous this place is at night?" He looked at her as disappointment filtered to his eyes.

"Shim don't bother with the anger, too much in one night will blow your mind."

"Too much in one night, too much what you talking about?" His voice had a tinge of evasiveness in it.

"Shim a heard the man threatening you." She stopped and allowed the statement to sink in. It had the desired effect as Shimron averted his eyes and stared overhead at the wall. "A heard him threaten you and a want to find out what you do to him." Martina stared fixedly at him, trying to get and hold his gaze.

"Tina don't bother yourself bout anything, jus' don't bother yourself. Don't pay idle, waste man any mind!" Again, he averted his eyes as if hers could pull his secret out and force him to talk.

Martina called his name, trying to force his attention

and the truth from him. "Shim if it is nothing or foolishness as you say then it is very easy for you to tell me. People hide things that are important, not things that are foolish." She was trying to corner him and loosen his tongue.

"Sis just leave it alone, a don't want you to get mix up. An' remember dat I don't want anybody at all to know you is my sister for more reason than one." She had Shimron's attention now because he looked straight into her eyes as if to concretize his warning.

"I can sort of understand that knowing how this world run, if anything should happen and you can't catch Kwako then you can catch him shut. But even that is suggestive and a need to know if you in any trouble. Please Shim tell me what going on," she pleaded, moving closer to him.

"But might as well yuh tell her; a don't see what you hiding, she need to know so she can protect herself and Yvette and Miss Turner."

Martina swung towards the voice which was coming from the room door. It was Shimron's girlfriend, Nadra. She was leaning against the door with her arms folded across her chest and fear forming in her globe eyes.

"Nadra why you not sleeping? You need to sleep when the baby sleeping so that you can get some rest." His voice held an edge of caring annoyance.

"Shim, sleep in the noise dat you making?" She yawned sleepily.

Shimron looked at his sister as if making up his mind and then said, "It is not everything woman should know.

The less you know about certain t'ings is the better for you but since you pressing me…" He stopped talking and looked away, as if he were alone in the room and did not remember them. He spun around suddenly as if he had decided to spill something hot and had to do it quickly. "Dem wretched criminal want mi fi join dem gang. They been bothering me for the last two months but no is not good enough for them so they keep annoying me. I put down badness an' a not taking it up again. A don't have a father an' I would love for my yute to have one. A don't want him to grow up witless an' wayward like me. Is only God why I living until today!" He pounded his palm with his fist and walked away and sat in a chair. His face was brutal and his eyes dead and defiant in the illuminating glare of the light bulb. Martina shivered inwardly, reflecting on Shimron's journey in crime and how he had almost been killed but had defied death and had been reformed. It would send her into a mental tailspin if he were to become involved in drug trafficking again.

"Shim a think we better find another place to live," Nadra said, sounding desperate and afraid. She did not want her son to grow up without a father like Shimron and herself had. Also, she had more than one reason for wanting to leave Port-Herb. She had been watching Bibi, a girl who had just left school, who lived about three houses away. She was obviously attracted to Shimron and kept parading in front of their house. As soon as Shimron came home each day, she would appear on the road in her barely there shorts which clung desperately to her skin almost suffocating it, and her mane of synthetic glory flaming down her back. At first Shimron appeared not to notice, but after the first few times she could see him casting furtive glances at the girl and smiling secretly to himself.

She was well aware of the culture of the inner city where males and relationships were concerned. It was the norm for them to have several women at the same time and sometimes beget many children. Then the women or 'baby mothers' as they were called would vie desperately for the man's attention and child maintenance, by becoming immersed in verbal and sometimes physical warfare for which you had to be equipped with caustic lengths of hardcore expletives and the ability to wield threats and fight with any effective missile of female destruction. The men in the interim exulting in their machismo, did very little to contain the constant confrontation between their 'baby mothers'. It gave them a false sense of importance to have the women wrangling over them. The only thing that was not to their liking was the child maintenance which some evaded with great skill.

Nadra, even though she was only a teenager, knew all about this only too well as her mother had been a six-time victim of absent fathers which had caused her children to be strangers to education and a friend of poverty and crime. Nadra wanted something better for herself but had not gone beyond grade eight in a primary and junior high school. However, she had vowed to herself that she would not emulate her mother and those of her siblings which had followed her. She had to find a way to go back to school or get a skill to help herself and as to having six children, no way! Not even a legion of the smoothest talking men could break her fierce resolve to not have more than two and not anywhere in the near future.

"Nadra you know we can't afford to live anywhere else right now cause of the money vibes. If a was getting job regular then we could a move to a better place where we could afford to pay the rent an' other bills but right now it not possible. Is me alone an' yuh know how things go. Moreover, a have to think about Tina, Yvette and Miss Turner." He paused and looked at Martina with brotherly concern pouring out of his eyes.

Martina looked back at him, returning the sentiment. Their mother would have been so proud of Shimron thinking about his siblings and not just himself. She also knew her mother would have wanted them to stay together, especially since her father was not around to help her anymore, but if Shimron was in trouble, this was not the place for him. These gang members were not people to play with, you either lived by their rules or leave before they liquidated you. Martina felt fear attacking her limbs, weakening them.

"Maybe you should talk to the area leader, I hear he tries to be fair to those who live around here," Martina suggested haltingly. She did not want Shimron to have even the remotest dealing with any questionable character, but if that would help them to give him a break, then she would encourage him to do it.

Shimron hissed his teeth and got up hurriedly, almost tipping over the chair. His face had a dour look with dark steely eyes fixed in front of him. He paced the floor and then stopped to shrug his shoulders uncertainly without speaking.

Back in her house Martina tried to put the whole incident out of her mind. As she did every night, she called her father's number hoping for a miracle in the form of a response. Instead of the usual voicemail, a clipped superficial voice announced that the number was no longer assigned. Martina closed her eyes as a feeling of despondency was born in her. It spread even more when she called his home and no one answered. She interpreted this to mean that the family was not back yet. They obviously did not want to become embroiled in her father's ordeal or perhaps they feared for their lives. The feelings of aloneness and anxiousness washed over her. She had to do what she had to do.

Five

Downtown Kingston was bustling with Monday morning activity. The regular vendors had snatched what rest they could on Sunday and were back at it early. It was only nine o'clock and already both sides of the streets were lined with vendors and their wares. There were carts laden with clothing, glassware, ground provision, jelly coconuts, shoes, biscuits, drink, soap powder and other washing agents, toiletries and if you could conceive it, it could be found. Some people did not set up any kind of permanent selling areas but walked around selling their wares or pushing small carts with bag juice, light snacks, underwear and other small items. They advertised their wares in crude, compelling, competitive tones which sounded intimidating rather than inviting.

"Bag juice me a sell! A de cheapest one round town; buy t'ree an' yuh get it at wholesale price!"

"Children brief an' panty, cover the pickney dem bottom fore dem ketch cole!"

"Irish mash an' linseed, strengthen yuh back so the black race can continue!" Everyone tittered at this and the man pushing the cart with the bottles laughed louder than everyone else, enjoying his own ribald joke.

The people's dress was as colourful and outrageous as their language; there were young men, many of them school age, wearing 'dog-bitten' jeans which glaringly exposed sections of their thighs and knees. These jeans dipped unceremoniously below the buttocks as if in disagreement with the waist or hips or as if in a forgetful moment, the owners had forgotten to put them back into place after using the toilet. This allowed everyone to view the underpants or shorts which gave way to the underwear's brand name. It seemed to be the order of the day, the dress code of the young and the thoughtless.

The girls on the other hand sported barely there brief-buttocks shorts which rode their bottoms like a saddle rides a horse, rocking to and fro with the motion of their movements. Both young and older women wore suffocating jeans or tights which clung to their cramped bodies; the cheeks of their buttocks begging for freedom and not trying in any way to stave off the lascivious leers of the male population.

Martina looked at everything like someone who had landed on planet Earth and was surveying the earthlings; like someone who was born and grown in the inner city but had somehow managed to be divorced from some of the appendages that came with it. She viewed it all with slight trepidation seeping into her limbs and causing her hands to quiver and her feet to develop an involuntary tremor which threatened to cast her on her face and humble her in front of all those aliens who seemed to be one with the incessant wave of noise and bustle that characterized the city.

Martina was standing in front of a group of stores which clung to one another like Siamese twins, different only in their physical appearance as it pertained to the paintwork, names and the amount of graffiti which was splattered all over the peeling scrolled paintwork. There was no allowance for breathing and where a line of buildings ended, a street began. A few hundred meters behind these buildings some taller buildings stretched themselves like giraffes, overshadowing and dwarfing the others, relegating them to garage-like status.

The cries of the vendors brought back Martina to the present and she stepped out of the way of an impatient vendor right into a small stream of water which seemed to be coming from further up the road and had carved out a route for itself by eating its way into the concrete at the side of the road in front of the shops. Light garbage flowed heedlessly along but heavier pieces got stuck in the crevices and impeded the flow of the lighter pieces which sometimes manoeuvred their way around them or fell in line behind the anchored pieces being buffeted and pushed but unable to gain their freedom. A close look revealed an area of green moss and slimy black substance clinging to the garbage. A purulent smell which Martina had failed to notice at first because of her discomfiture and state of uncertainty, wafted its way to her nostrils and assaulted her senses. She stepped out of the way of a vendor and stepped right into the scorned water.

She made a sound of surprised disgust, held her bag closely to her and tried to get out of the crowd, shaking her foot like a salt shaker to get rid of the clinging putrefying scent. She knew she would need some water to wash her feet as a foul smell would only be an obstacle for what she wanted to do. She searched carefully around for a pipe but found none and ended up buying a bottle of water. In a strange way, this diversion was a way of delaying her purpose and even though she did not like the type of distraction, she welcomed the playing for time, the pushing back of the moment, the brief suspension of the time of decision, the postponing of the actual time of action. She poured the water on her feet slowly, deliberately, purposefully, as if every gush, every stream, every trickle, every drop aided and abetted her delaying tactic.

Having finished her activity, she stood upright and clutched the huge, thick, transparent plastic bag to her as if it somehow held comforting virtues and had become a physical crutch for her indecision. She was standing in the park and from there she saw what seemed to be the hub of activity. There were buses streaming in and rushing out, people embarking and disembarking hurriedly, some lackadaisically, people moving seemingly to work, business or leisure, their movements denoting the pulsating throb and heartbeat of the city. The other motor vehicles joined in with the motion and the rhythm with their sporadic, erratic dash and impatient blaring of horns. Martina decided that the overly crowded area was not for her. She was not exactly streetwise nor did she want to meet anyone she knew from her past life; remaining incognito was her objective.

Martina felt that her procrastination was pointless. She had to do what she had to do and fumbling with fear and indeterminate indecision were not necessarily a part of her character. She would not survive if she were a weakling, things were far from how she had planned them but she had no one so she had to do what she could for Yvette, Miss Turner and herself. Despite her resolve, sweat rose up unbidden and soaked her palms and her forehead and then ran hurriedly down her face as if it too wanted to hide from the rest of the world. She assisted in its disappearance by sweeping it swiftly to the side of her face.

Ten minutes later she crossed the street and walked down to an area where a number of people were coming and going. There was a vendor there bawling out his wares:

"See di CD dem yah! The latest movie an' dancehall t'ing! See dem over yah so!

Buy dem fi yuh later when yuh cock up yuh foot in yuh living room!

See di CD dem yah!"

The vendor was dressed in a knee-length blue body-clinging frayed-foot jeans and a sleeveless vest to match. Despite herself, Martina felt a bubble rising in her stomach.

It surged upward and made its way to her throat and then tickled her throat and eyes. This was so because the young man's hair was cut in a Mohawk and was dyed in at least six different colours with matching beads anchored in different areas. The exposed area of his body in unity with his hair, had tattoos of different kinds of symbols criss-crossing and falling over one another. He gave Martina the chills and she immediately nicknamed him Tattoo Dye.

Tattoo Dye was a few feet away from another vendor who was selling costume jewellery. She used her mouth and her body as effective means of advertising.

"If you want fi look good come over here suh. Mi have everyt'ing dat yuh need fi look fine an' dandy; everyt'ing fi mek yuh pretty even if yuh hugly!" She tittered at her own joke and her front gold teeth joined in the joke by sparkling and shimmering brightly. Other parts of her body joined in the advertisement: at the front of her synthetic mane there was an imitation gold band; her ears were pierced in several places and a confusion of earrings dotted and dangled from the semi-circles that were her ears. Several small flat earrings had been forced into several places on her face including her upper and lower lips and her eyebrows. Her nose, not to be excluded, had a small red hoop hanging from the bridge. She was wearing a tight red halter top which allowed everyone to view the silver hoop swinging from her navel and the one dangling from the centre of her lower back. The back ring was placed amidst the tattooed name DONNETTE. Her fingers, hands and ankles further bore the burden of her trade with bangles, bracelets and anklets. Martina secretly called her Display Board.

Martina stopped a little distance from the vendors and leaned against the building for support. It was now or never, already she had left things far too late, who knew if she would have made a few dollars already. Like a suicide bomber or one bearing a weapon of mass destruction, she hesitantly pulled the clean, transparent plastic bag from the one she was carrying. The bright colours in the bag mocked her unhappy mood. Then, "Bag juice, banana chips and sweetie" a voice from somewhere inside squeaked softly. She literally jumped at the sound of her voice; she couldn't believe it had come out of her. She turned away from the faces that looked at her momentarily as if to find the culprit who had spoken. Sweat watered her face and palms, and again she welcomed the diversion and swept the water away nonchalantly.

"Bag juice! Banana chips! Sweetie!" the voice came again, less timorous but with a hesitant tremor. She felt the water well in her face, formed small bubbles, broke and then streamed heedlessly down her face and then dripped noiselessly on the bag juice bag as if it did not want to betray her.

Nobody stopped but Tattoo Dye and Display Board looked openly at Martina, not in a hostile manner but with a kind of questioning curiosity. They were accustomed to seeing new vendors on the street but there was something odd about this young girl, Donnette thought. She looked at her from head to toe taking note of the short processed hair caught in one with a pony clip, the frightened saturnine face, the milo-complexion, ordinary jeans which faintly outlined a figure which had potential to develop into something more than eye-catching a few years later. But it was not the physical appearance that struck her that much because once in a while you saw an ordinary young girl who seemed not to be chasing 'hotness', it was the voice that seemed too smooth, too cultured, too out of place for the downtown setting. This girl was definitely not downtown material, what was she doing here? She must have fallen on hard times. She thought of chasing her away to another section, but something stopped her. After all she was not selling the same things she and Tony were selling. She looked at her again and noticed the sad, indecisive look. "I wonder what her story is?" she wondered aloud, turning back to her wares.

Tattoo Dye looked at her inquisitively. She was not his type and even though some of the 'hot girls' were like clashing cymbals, loud, noisy and showy, he liked the excitement. He hoped she was not planning to stay there too long. Her face was too serious and shy. Something about her was out of place but that was not his business. He just wanted to sell and chat up the 'hot' girls hoping that one would talk to him seriously. His child's mother was working on the other side of town so he could take his chances.

After ten minutes of calling out occasionally, Martina had her first customers. It was a mother and her two children and they bought both bag juice and banana chips. Even though it was only a little more than a hundred dollars, Martina felt a sense of achievement. She had really sold something and as yet nobody had cursed her or chased her away and she had not seen anybody that she knew. She had not told anyone at home what she was up to. She had lied to Miss Turner and Yvette when she told them that she had a job downtown selling products for a company. She had bought a few cheap items to place on top of the bag in case their curiosity was piqued and they opened the bag. She would buy the bag juice from the company each morning and what was left over she would hide it in the refrigerator and even give them a few sometimes. She did not like the deception because she knew Miss Turner and Shimron would object but what could she do? She had to pay the bills and send Yvette to school. She hoped she would make enough at least five days for the week. Saturdays would be optional because she needed time to rest. Standing on her feet and bawling out her wares for hours would certainly prove taxing and she wanted to still help Yvette with her school work.

It was not only Yvette that required her help but also two little girls who would be doing the primary school exit exam soon. Martina had no way of knowing how news of her ability had spread but the parents of the two little girls, Maria and Sheena, had come knocking and asked her to help them and she did not have the heart to say no. She had warned them not to tell anyone else as she did not have more than one and a half hours each evening.

Sheena and Maria's parents were not the only ones who had come knocking and asking. About four houses down the road there lived a little seven-year-old girl. She had the most alluring black eyes staring innocently out of a globular chocolate face. Her sunflower smile warmed not only the atmosphere around her but sent rays into the heart, but alas, she was born hopelessly lame in her right foot and could only drag it unwillingly along as she walked. Her parents did not see the necessity of sending her to school beyond grade two. They claimed the other children made fun of her and that prevented her from learning but Martina found that the child had a sharp mind and was eager to learn. Again, she had no idea how she had found out about her as the only contact they had had was her calling shyly out to her when she was passing by her house and then going indoors to hide her boldness. She hoped that she would not be too tired after the sun had seeped into her skin and drained her of her energy.

She would just have to see how that worked out, right now survival was beckoning and she had to try and get enough sales to exist on.

"My girl, yuh have to walk roun' sometimes an' try sell," Display Board advised. "After yuh get used to the place yuh will learn which part fi go sell," she continued, looking Martina up and down. She felt a pull towards the nervous, uncertain girl. There was something out of place about her. Her mind went into active mode, mapping out her own story of her life – parents poor, drop out of school, absent father, not so street smart. Well, she will soon learn the tricks of the trade if she stick aroun' long enough, she mused. Somehow a don't t'ink she going to last long, a little too polish.

Martina did not know what to think of Display Board but she appreciated the advice. At that moment, she felt no urge to walk, she would just see how things worked out and observe as she went along. She sold a few more items in the morning, noting that bag juice seemed to be the more desired item and that it was mainly the children who purchased from her. There were a large number of them out of school and Martina knew their story only too well, hadn't she gone through it before – little or no food to eat, unemployed parents, no lunch money, no books, cramped living space, under-aged girls and boys abandoned into their own care. No one seemed to care, high authority hounded you into the earth if one died, but did not really care how they lived. They didn't seem to care much for the mentally ill and dispossessed, from where she was standing she could see a few of them lying on the pavement or walking around begging or scrounging like dogs for discarded leftovers in the garbage. Some carried their few possessions in black scandal bags or in bundles in their hands or on their backs. Two of them had passed her, lost in a world peopled only by themselves, their faces blackened by accumulated dirt, furrowed by lines of pain and hardship, and dazed by the sun and unfocused thoughts.

A lump grew in her throat and she swallowed, trying to bury it. Why did life have to be so sad for some people while others were enjoying the fruits of the Garden of Eden? Some might be responsible for their condition but others had it thrust upon them like the destructive acts of nature, sometimes sudden and unbidden. She thought about her own situation, all she needed was a chance in life to make her way. She wasn't asking for hand-outs, but the chance had been snatched from her while it was within grasp. Martina did not want to become locked in self-pity and wallow in the mire of misfortune; she had to fight her way out of poverty and she was determined to do this whatever it took.

That first day she hardly moved from that position, she took in all that she saw and put them away neatly in her mind for further thought and assessment. The noonday sun bore down on her like an enemy and sucked the energy out of her body. It fuelled her hunger and she crouched in front of the building and ate from her stock of items. She was careful not to eat too much although she was hungry because she needed to sell the items to get the money so she could live. She was glad that she had worn her hat and had wrapped the bag juice in newspaper as the scorching sun seemed bent on liquefying them both.

After she had eaten her meagre fare, she tried to attract more customers. She got only a few because there were quite a number of vendors moving around and selling the same items. She had not taken too much on the first day as she wanted to see how the sales would go. Also, she did not want to take home the extras and raise eyebrows about her job.

During the course of the day, a few street people stopped by to beg. Martina became even more aware of the fact that there were people who were worse off than she was; at least she was trying not to find herself in their position but fate had fixed their destiny, or so it seemed, and so they had no option. Their eyes were so full of sadness and one could not fail to see the hunger hacked deep into their faces. The desperation with which they begged, tugged at the strings of her heart. She knew what it was like to be hungry and the hopelessness which came with it so she gave them what she could knowing that it didn't even begin to assuage the hunger purposefully, painfully poking daggers of pain in all sections of your anatomy and then sending the electrifying signals to the brain causing desperation, disorientation and distress.

There was one particular vagrant who had interested her. She had noticed him sitting across the road on the piazza of a department store. He had not moved from that position in hours and she wondered if he were ill. Even though he was sitting she could see that he was a tall man. She wondered if he was new to the downtown life and was taking it all in before immersing himself into the thick of things. She had made up her mind not to give away any more items but decided that if he came over, she would oblige him. Minutes before she left, she noticed that he was standing and was attempting to cross the road. He did not step out into the road like somebody who was mentally ill but waited until the road was clear. He was favouring his left foot but his gait was not slow. He seemed to be making straight for her, but changed course at the last minute. Then he appeared to have targeted her and ambled towards her.

He stopped a little from her and she pretended not to

notice. He shuffled up to her and stopped about three feet away. Her eyes were drawn to his face but he held his head down as if he did not want to stare into her eyes. She waited until he approached her directly and then she tried to look more closely at him when he stretched out his hand, palm upwards, eyes lowered under the long cap front. Martina tried not to stare too much and took her time to reach into her bag to give him the items. He lifted his eyes to her face as she hesitated and she got her chance to look. His face looked taut and drawn, almost like the skin had been stretched over it like the face of a drum or like he had had a skin graft. He had a mud-coloured complexion and his eyes were sunken, almost lost in his eye sockets. He was wearing a blue long-sleeve tee shirt and a tired but clean blue jeans pants. Martina held back her hand, listening for his voice, but only a dumb show – gestures without speech – followed.

"He can't talk," Tattoo Dye volunteered, looking on with interest. "Him come bout a few times since last month but him nuh talk at all, but yuh know that him can hear cause when you ask him anything him shake him head."

"A wonda what really happen to him?" Display Board asked and without waiting for an answer she said, "It must be something really dramatic an' him tek it real bad for it to dramatize him so."

Martina hid her smile in a yawn, said goodbye to the two and walked towards the bus stop.

Six

It was 7:30, Martina had just finished helping the girls and they had just gone home. She had watched them from the front door making certain that they reached home safely. The week before there had been a report of a teenage girl going missing and no one was certain whether she had run away or had been taken away. Lately, there had been much talk about human trafficking. The male predators were on the prowl, preying on the unsuspecting young girls, enticing them with so called easy money and a glamorous lifestyle. Many of the girls were tired of poverty and saw it as a way out. They were so enthralled about earning money and managing their own life they had no idea that they were helping to reinvent slavery by becoming willing pawns. It was more like assisting the slave buyers to put shackles of misery and pain around them. On the other hand, there were the unsuspecting who were captured and sold into the sex trade, their only hope, like the slaves of yore, was escape or death.

Martina had noticed that Yvette seemed to be changing. Her shuttered personality was opening a little. She had made friends with two girls in the community, Karina Brown and Jessica Tomlin, who attended the same school as she did. Although Martina was happy that Yvette's social life had received a boost, there was something about the girls that she was not comfortable with. They had visited on two occasions and Martina had overheard an unsavoury conversation and had peeped at a picture which they had been circulating among themselves. She had spoken to Yvette about these things when the girls were gone.

"Yvette, I am happy that you are getting over your problems," she started out, going to sit beside her as she lay on the bed with the television watching her because her eyes were locked on the phone which she hastily turned over when Martina sat next to her. Martina took note and continued, "Yvette there is something about those girls I don't like. The things I overheard you talking about the other day did not sound right at all. A want you to be careful." She looked directly at Yvette who turned her face away and then right back at her sister.

"What problem you have with me an' my friends? If a stay by myself you say a too droopy an' withdrawn, a shutting down like shame mi lady macka. If a talk to people now you have a problem." She hissed her teeth rudely and shuffled away from Martina.

"Yvette, listen to mi," Martina pleaded, touching Yvette on her shoulder. She was a little shocked when she felt her pull away as if repulsed by her touch. "Yvette, as far as I know you are the only sister a have. I am the oldest and since we have no mother I am in charge of you." She swallowed hard as she mentioned her mother. It was almost three years now but the wounds opened up by her mother's death had not closed; they were still raw and running like a putrefied sore. Her father's disappearance and probable death which might mean she was an orphan only widened the wound.

"Yvette you remember that you have no mother and father. Remember that you have to try your best to lift yourself out of this poverty and the wrong company can't help you. Education is a way out and you must try and at least finish high school. I –"

"What?" Yvette sprung to a sitting position like a spring that had been scrunched and then suddenly released. She looked at Martina as if she had suddenly gone mad. "Which education? You turn idiot? Look how much subject you have an' not just some little fool fool pass, an' you can't even get a job in a store!" She laughed mockingly, shaking her body, especially her head, in derision.

Martina felt the blow like a boxer's punch below the waist. How much did Yvette know about her downtown enterprise? Had she managed to fool her? "Yvette, because I can't find a good job now don't mean that a not going to get one at all." Talk about encouraging one's self, or was it a deferred dream that she hoped would be realized one day when some things changed in Jamaica.

"Tina, continue to fool yourself if you want to. We are lower class people an' we have to live in our lower-class kingdom an' leave big high-up people in their own world." She was emphatic, unmoving in her views.

"So why do you bother to go to school then?" Martina threw back at her, hoping to stump her.

"Well," Yvette fired back, all gassed. "I don't want anybody to write my name pan any bulla an' I eat it an' don't know that is my name. If yuh can't read an' write an' don't have a little sense in dis world then yuh really salt. But I not going to fancy myself in a world a don't belong to. I going to find other means to live."

"Like going downtown to sell bag juice for your whole life?" Martina said, inwardly reeling from the backlash of her own words. Wasn't that what she was doing now? She assured herself that she was not going to be in that business venture for too long. It was only a temporary measure. Do or die, she, Martina Patterson was going to go to university and graduate and get one of those so-called upper class jobs and show the world that she was a person too!

"Well a don't know that selling bag juice is a crime. Many people do it an' police see them an' don't lock dem up!" Yvette said brusquely, turning her back rudely to her sister.

"Yvette have some manners! We come from the lower class but our mother teach us good manners so don't turn your back to me! I am responsible for you and if you get yourself into trouble a have to be there for you, so know your place!" Martina was trying not to shout or hit Yvette but the temptation was very strong.

"A know Tina but yuh can't hit me, yuh not mi mother an' a certainly entitled to my own opinion an' my own friends!" She got off the bed and went towards the front door in a huff. Her face bore the black threatening look of an approaching thunderstorm.

"A hope yuh not planning to go anywhere out of the house at this time," Martina said, trying to assert her authority. "This is not a place for you to be walking around in the night, moreover what would you be doing outside at this time of night? This is a part of the inner city you know." She walked towards her, hoping to deter her, but Yvette got to the door before her, opened it and stepped outside.

"Yvette come back inside this minute! Miss Turner! Miss Turner!" Martina yelled, rushing into Miss Turner's room like a sweeping tide. "Miss Turner! Miss Turner!"

"What happen Tina girl?" Miss Turner asked, awakening from her sleep and looking around her dazed as if she were in strange surroundings.

"Miss Turner, Yvette gone outside in the night and a try to stop her but she don't pay me any mind. She get real feisty and out of order these days," Martina reported.

Miss Turner crinkled her wrinkled face and the network of wrinkles crisscrossed even more. Martina was sorry she had woke her up because her age was beginning to take its toll; arthritis, high blood pressure and diabetes were now her constant companions. She shied away from the idea that one day she would be gone from them.

"How yuh mean she gone out in the dark?" Miss Turner asked incredulously, getting off the bed in her fastest slowtime. "How yuh mean she gone off in the night, is who send her?"

"She gone by herself. She tek up with bad company and them leading her astray. Miss Turner if you ever hear how she argue with me a while ago!" Martina's voice held disbelief at Yvette's temerity.

"Oh God suppose them rape her an' abduct her like the little girl dat disappear last week?" Miss Turner's voice held fear, real fear grounded in what was happening in the society and even greater fear because Martina had had a close call and Yvette herself had been a victim. Another incident like that would probably push her over the cliff.

"How long she gone Tina? How long she gone?" Miss Turner sounded like a tape recorder.

"About five minutes ago she just walk through the door like she a big woman who own her own house and have her own key!" Martina was still smarting at the rebuff dealt to her by her younger sister.

"We have to get Shim to help us," Miss Turner suggested, hobbling towards the door.

"No Miss Turner you sit down. A will get Shim, don't bother yourself," Martina said, holding Miss Turner's hand and leading her to sit at the table. "Don't take up too much stress on your head, remember the high blood pressure. A don't want you in the hospital. A was wrong to wake you up at all." She waited until Miss Turner had settled into the chair before going next door. Seeking help from Shimron was something she was hesitant about. She had not heard anything else about the gang's threat and she was reluctant to ask him about it, but she knew he would not be too happy to go out into the night. There were a number of lanes leading off the main road and in each lane danger lurked like a wild cat in the jungle waiting to spring. Moreover, where would they find Yvette? Port-Herb was not exactly a small place and she could be anywhere. Maybe she was just gone to visit her friends and there was no real cause for worry, she reasoned to herself.

Shimron peeped through the window to assure himself of the caller and then on recognizing Martina, opened the door immediately. Even before she stated the purpose for her visit, concern lined his face and clouded his eyes. He seemed to live with the expectancy of trouble; his body was taut, ready to spring, poised for action.

"Tina what's the matter?" he asked as soon as he had closed the door behind her.

Martina noted the coiled look and tried to joke a bit. "Is that how you greet me? Couldn't I just be paying you a sisterly visit to see how you are?"

"Yes yuh could, but not at night an' not when your knock sound like a rent collector, bailiff or a police." He tried to smile but something inside pulled it back in its formative stage and instead his permanent aura fell back in place.

Martina decided not to hold back anymore. "Shim a really come for help or advice about Yvette." She started slowly and then rushed off the sentence like water gushing from a pipe.

"Hold on Tina, hold on girl. What happen to Yvette an' where she gone?" Shimron asked, anxiously facing Martina.

"A don't know she left in a huff and a come to ask for help to find her or for you to tell me what you think I should do," Martina blurted out desperately.

"Find her? A wouldn't know where to look an' maybe she gone to one of the girls a see her parring with these days. A was happy she was finally coming out of her shell but it look like dem not the right company." Shimron's lips were twitching and his eyes blinked incessantly. "A not going out there, mainly because a don't know where to start looking an' the next t'ing it not safe for me or you out there. Yuh know there are some places around here that yuh just can't go to or else they will say yuh spying an' shoot yuh." His voice was frank, matter of fact, final.

"A really don't blame you Shim and I understand the danger. A know I will never be able to sleep until she come home. A just hope she comes early and in one piece. A really going read her some rules tonight!" Martina was struggling to keep calm, but it was difficult. Of all the problems she had thought about, a problem of this nature with Yvette had never entered her mind.

"A think a know where she gone," a voice announced behind them.

They both spun around in the direction of the voice. It was Nadra. She had a habit of emerging from the room to join in conversations. She was holding the baby on her shoulder, but he was restive and kept moving about like a plant being blown by the wind.

"And how would you know bout dat?" Shimron questioned curiously, flames in his eyes. "How would you know?"

Nadra looked away from him and pinpointed Martina with her gaze. "Tina all the craze round here is a new night club dat dem open down di road an' then round the corner. All the young girl dem either go round there to dance or look." Her face was triumphant with the knowledge that she had been the one to impart the information.

Shimron glared at her, sending out questioning signals. "How you know about all dis? Where yuh go during the days when a go to work? What yuh do with the baby?"

"Yuh just asking me all dat cause yuh know dat you men love dat kind a t'ing. If I wasn't here maybe you would be round there now. Your girlfriend next-door a dance round there now, so yuh should know about that." She looked at him accusingly, watching the play of emotion on his face. He was trying to control the slight tremor of his lips by biting down on it. Nadra watched him like a cat watching a saucer of milk about to be had by another cat. The girl, Bibi, who had been flirting with him had been giving her the "I have him too" look whenever she went outside with her baby. She suspected that even though she had seen no changes in Shimron he had somehow found a way to be unfaithful. She told herself it was the way of the inner city, but she had somehow hoped that Shimron would be different.

"Which girlfriend Nad? Which girlfriend? Strange dat yuh trying to fine woman give me, a think it would be the other way around! What I have to do with nite club? Tell me, a really interested to hear an' not just dat, how you know so much bout night club round the corner?" He advanced towards her in a timely, threatening manner, demanding an answer.

Nadra stood her ground and looked straight at him. Her mother had told her once that if a woman appeared to be afraid of a man, he would always take advantage of her, crush her in every way and always continue to beat her. She knew it was the norm in some homes but she was not going to allow it even though she was shaking like jelly inside. Shimron really towered over her in terms of height and she was like a fly to his size.

"Everybody round here know about the night club. These houses rub one another cheek to cheek an' unless you whisper, everybody can hear what everybody else say in their house. Everybody know when yuh use the bathroom. Everybody know when yuh quarrel, who get beaten from who don't, everything, jus' everything. An' if yuh stay in here a daytime yuh can hear all the gossip without even going outside, an' I go out sometimes. The food don't get buy an' come to me by itself, an' bills don't pay themselves an'–"

"Just remember who yuh talking to girl, a don't like yuh tone at all. It sound feisty an' you not going to be feisty to me, just remember dat I wear the boxers in dis house." He looked at her as if he wanted to hit her and Martina stepped in to diffuse the situation.

"Please, please stop the quarrelling! A didn't come over here for this. A just need some help to know what to do, not to have us quarrelling with each other, which will only create more problems." Martina stepped between them and held up her hands. Shimron stared fixedly at her for a while, thinking, contemplating and then he cast knife-point glances at Nadra and walked away.

Martina still did not know what to do. One thing she was certain of was that Shimron would not be helping her to find Yvette. He had made that clear and under the circumstances she agreed with him, but what was she to do? The best thing was to sit up and wait, but what was she going to say to her when she turned up? She had no doubt that she would turn up, when was the question.

She left the house with Shimron promising to watch out for Yvette and at the same time telling Martina that in case he fell asleep she should call him whatever time she came in. Shimron waited at the door until she was safely inside and then locked his door.

Martina sat at the table and tried to read a book but she could not concentrate and her thoughts drifted with all the clouds which clouded her life: Where was her father? Was he still alive? All calls to his cell phone still went unanswered. How would people from her old life react when they heard of her new business enterprise? Who could she go to for help with Yvette? Should she really open up and tell Leonie and Andre what had been happening to her? She could not lie and say that her two friends had not tried to find out about her but she did not want them to know about her present state. She felt like a balloon which had been inflated and was riding in the wind only for a malicious bird to come along and pierce it with its beak, sending it spluttering and doddering back to earth in pieces. She did not think they were disingenuous as their calls really sounded desperate for news but she did not want them to see that she had returned to her lowly state. When she had found a way out she would call them, not now.

She fell into a fitful doze and was awakened by an impatient knock on the door. She listened again and the knock was repeated accompanied by Yvette's surly voice. Now who should sound unfriendly, Martina questioned? Who told her to be outdoors at this time of night? She checked the time as she made her way slowly, purposely to the door. Let her stew in her own discomfort, at eleven o'clock nobody told her to be outside.

Martina opened the door slowly and Yvette pushed her way in followed by a fuming Shimron. So that was why she had been so impatient! Shimron had really waited up. She tried to push past Martina as if she were a bundle to be tossed aside but Martina stood her ground and almost toppled over.

Yvette stood upright and shot darts at Martina with her glance. "Why yuh have to stand in the way when yuh see me passing?"

"Stand in your way, I was only opening the door which I shouldn't have and you almost pushed me down, very good manners!"

"Yuh have a nerve!" Shimron chimed in. "Coming in here when duppy fraid an' arguing with people. Where yuh coming from an' who tell yuh dat yuh could go out in the night?" Shimron's voice was not loud, but it held a deadly steel-like quality.

Yvette cringed but decided to bluff her way out. "A jus' went down the road with my friends. Anything wrong with dat? An' a old enough to go out!"

"Yes you can go out now and again but not at night and not with those friends! Where did you go?" Martina blocked her way as she tried to sail around her.

Shimron went and stood in front of her, blocking her completely. "Yuh turn big woman now going out at night! Dat mean yuh must have yuh own place an' key. How come yuh jus' change all of a sudden? Is what get into yuh head?" Sparks of anger flew from the steely voice.

"How come the two a yuh jus' a attack mi suh, especially you Shim? Yuh memba how yuh use to give mummy trouble day an' night an' sometimes nobody don't see yuh for days? An' the one night mi jus' go round the corner yuh behaving like His Righteousness!" Yvette voice was rising rapidly with the current of her fury. She placed her arms akimbo and glowered unblinkingly at her brother.

For a moment, her action reminded Yvette of their mother, loud, forthright and brazen, always firing back in confrontations, never given to listening and discussing amicably.

Shimron looked at Yvette long and hard before answering. She sensed his anger rising like a tsunami and again she cowered inwardly, waiting to be slapped. She stood in sullen silence and waited for him to act because she could not run away as he was blocking her completely.

He advanced until he was only inches away from her and in a calm, controlled voice he addressed her, "Yvette, yes a give my mother trouble; yes a stop going to school; yes a smoke weed; yes a delivered drugs; yes a get shot; an' yes a learn mi lesson! Only a fool would not learn a lesson from all dat! A still have mi bad ways but a learn to leave badness an' illegal runnings alone. A living by the sweat of my brow, is not much but when a get a job a try an' make two ends meet. Mummy dead but a swear she would want me to take care of you all an' dat is what a trying to do. Try finish school, don't be like me cause a regret it! Even if I couldn't get a job like how Tina can't find a decent one, I would have more education in mi head an' less people would try to mek fool out of me. Check the boy dem who come a try get mi into gang, if I did educated they wouldn't try it, but because dem know that mi don't have much book sense dem a try get mi into gang. No way, dem have to shoot mi again but this time is for something good! An' what mi a try say to yuh is dat yuh must finish school an' try an' mek something good out of your life, it can't be that we going to stay this way in life forever. I aim to get out, Tina aim to get out an' yuh mus' try an' mek it out!" This might have been the longest speech that Shimron had ever made in his life but he must have felt honour bound to make it.

Martina looked at him with pride, knowing their mother would have been so proud that Shimron had come into his own as a man. "Yvette all you need to do is listen and learn and try and bear it until things get better. That's all we are saying to you," she pleaded, reaching out a hand to Yvette who ignored it as if a fly of no consequence had perched beside her.

"I was really going to give yuh a beaten but yuh lucky a in mi good mood. But guess what if yuh ever walk out of this place in the night again without permission yuh will really get it! Memba say mi tell yuh dat!" He looked at her hoping the words would fall on fertile soil and then he left without another word.

Yvette gave his retreating back a hostile look and rushed out of the room as if being pushed by a force.

Seven

It was three weeks since Martina had been selling in downtown, Kingston. She was still trying to learn the tricks of the trade, but that was not as important to her as all she wanted to do was sell enough so she could get the bills paid and feed her family. She was diffident about becoming a professional at it and was optimistic that somewhere, somehow her tenure would not last long. It was an onerous task to walk around and stand in the pelting, punishing sun whose only aim was to drain all the moisture from your body and leave you sagging and drooping like a feeble plant fighting the onslaught of the heat. She started to think about her aspiration and how she was going to achieve it. She would sell and save some money for her lunch money and bus fare and then borrow from Students' Loan Association; and while she was studying she would try to get a part-time job on campus, this would help with Yvette and Miss Turner.

Martina was so caught up in her reverie that she did not see him until he was a few feet away. She had no idea why she chose to focus on the person approaching, but her eyes caught the blue and grey Jordans, half smothered by black jeans, blue polo shirt with the heron crest and Faculty of Law written under it and then up to a youthful, attractive, dark brown face, sporting a new growth of hair on the chin and on the sides of the face. Martina reeled with shock but collected herself just in time to turn her back and flatten herself in a close embrace with the wall she was standing next to. She remained there for more than a minute, barely seeming to breathe while her heart protested strongly by pounding against her chest, trying to find a way out like she was doing.

She slowly turned around to find some people who were standing nearby surveying her in questioning silence. She felt the eyes boring, probing and digging into her, wanting to find out if she were ill or more exciting, having a mental fallout. It was funny, but people even though they could be sympathetic somehow had this unexplained yearning for the macabre, the bizarre or the supernatural. It piqued their interest, giving them material for gossip and an occasion to 'draw long bench' and palaver. She held her head down and pretended not to see them. She also tried to shut out the whiff of conversation which wafted its way to her: "A get off", "Pregnant", "A wonder what her problem is?" One middle-aged woman filled with maternal instinct came over and touched her. "Child is what happen? Yuh sick or what, come out the sun." Her voice held compassion and concern.

"I'm okay a just feel a little funny," the half lie came out, hastily, forced.

"Just sit down a little," the woman insisted. She reached out a helping hand.

"I'm all right, honestly, a soon feel better," Martina tried to convince her. "Thanks anyway."

When the curious bystanders had shaken their heads and cemented their comments about her state, she walked away from the spot and went and sat on the steps of one of the older buildings where fewer people were passing. She collected her thoughts and reflected on her near discovery. The young man was Andre, Andre Depass! What was he doing downtown? He was certainly not a downtown person! And to think he almost came upon her without her noticing him! What would she have said to him or he to her if he had seen her? She would just faint or run away. Andre was the only male she had ever given a serious thought; in fact they had been more than platonic friends in sixth form. She did not have a problem then because even though he was predominantly middle-class, she could say she had a little touch of class because of her father. Now there was no father, no room in a middle-class community, no university, no good job; only a small space in the inner city and eking out a living from selling on the street. She would be completely mortified and would come up with some excuse if he had seen her. She had told herself he must have moved on by now as there were any number of girls at the university where she knew he was studying. Why would he want to have anything to do with a downtown street vendor? The calls she had received from him must have been courtesy calls.

She was so intensely locked in her thoughts that she did not see the man who had crept up beside her until he spoke.

"What a gwaan my girl, yuh tek weh yuhself from the heat an' noise?"

Martina jumped and pulled herself from her introspection. "Yes I'm cooling off." She surveyed the man from his feet up; blue denim, red tee shirt with Aeropostale splashed across the front, one huge, work-toughened palm stretched towards her; the other hand held a large transparent bag with undefined goods in it. Her eyes travelled to his face and she saw the dome-shaped scar which arched from one side of his cheek to the other. Hair sprouted from it helping to form his beard. His eyes were aflame and watery and had a hungry watchful gaze.

She jumped up and moved away from him. He was not mentally unstable, but she did not like how he looked at her.

"What happen young girl, yuh fraid a mi? A notice yuh from the other day an' a t'ink we would make a nice couple. A have two stalls an' somebody a work for me. Yuh wouldn't have to come out here on the street a hustle so hard. What yuh t'ink?" His eyes had the greed of an animal whetting his appetite for prey.

"Yes you have two stalls and six women, satisfy with that!" Martina flung her words at him and made her way across the road, walking between the parked vehicles without looking back. This was happening on an almost daily basis and she wondered if these men didn't have anything to do except hound young girls whom they thought were all out looking for men. It brought her back to the man who had approached her the Friday before just as she got off the bus and was walking towards home. He invited himself as her walking partner and sidled up close to her. She was afraid of some of the men in the community so she walked along pretending not to see him, holding her head straight and upright as if there were a heavy block cast in mortar on her shoulder.

"My girl stop a little an' talk to me nuh," he started.

Martina continued down the street without answering or acknowledging him in any way. The heavy thud of his boots clumped along beside her lighter steps. His rude, hoarse tone rolled out inflicting her eardrums.

"My girl yuh look well an' it look like yuh nuh have nuh yute yet, a full time now. Yuh must older than fifteen an' yuh should have at least two yute by now. A why you a play like yuh nuh know what woman in this world for." His annoying growl irritated her even more. She knew that all the men in the community were not like him, but right now she just hated them all.

Martina forgot her resolve and whirled around to face the heavy, beefy, early forties man. "Why don't you go and take care of the whole heap a pickney and ton load a baby mother that you already have? There are other things in life more than having baby before you're ready. Leave me alone and go mine the pickney dem that you have already!"

The man stopped walking and looked at her with

astonishment on his face. At first, he did not say anything and by the time he had decided what to say, Martina was quite a few yards away from him when he found the words. "Gwaan wid yuh big talk, yuh business soon fix, watch!"

She did not answer him but the veiled threat in his voice did not fail to reach her and fear rose in her for two reasons. The first one was that she did not like how some of the men in the community looked at her; their silence did not allay her negative opinion of them. The second reason was that if they thought you were behaving out of context with the other women, they would try to break you in. Martina was becoming more and more uncomfortable and the worst thing about it was that right now she was caught in a bind like an animal in a trap with no way out; she had nowhere else to live.

Martina went to a different location where there were more people, where she would not stand out and where she could easily disappear in a crowd. The only negative was that most of them were vendors and that was bad for business. Instead of shouting out she simply stood by and hoped the customers would patronize her. By the end of the day she had sold off everything so she was happy about that.

The following day she went down early, got her goods and went to the same location she had been the day before. She was not the only one who was out early, the street was almost full, and the vendors were setting out their wares – spreading sheets, thick plastic or tarpaulin on the sidewalk and then displaying their goods on them. Martina surveyed the many vendors and the same thought she had the first day she ventured downtown was the same one she had now. There were so many vendors, how did they all hope to survive by selling when they were more than the buyers? Miss Turner would say, water more than flour. There seemed to be even more that day and Martina's fervent prayer was that someday soon she would be out of that fray.

The morning was the same as usual, as it settled down to the sound of vendors hawking their wares, the hubbub of noise coming from the screaming sound-boxes and the never-ending swish, splutter and screech of motor vehicles. Martina was making moderate sales, at the same time watching out for anyone from her former upscale life. It was really a distracting bother and she started thinking about job-hunting again.

She was not prepared for what happened next. "Run! Run! Dem a come, the metro beast dem a come!" This came from a vendor whose goods were occupying a part of the road designated for driving; most of the vendors had their goods in the road.

The warning reverberated throughout the street and was echoed by the others. "The metro beast dem a come! Move it fast!" There was a whirl and a flurry of activities as the vendors hurriedly folded up their sheets and tarpaulin and sprinted as if all things dangerous in the world were chasing them. In the melee that ensued, some people were pushed over and goods that were not removed in the rush were trampled. There were curses and screams and cries of pain as the "beasts" descended upon the fleeing vendors, blocking those they could and confiscating what they could. The vendors who were adversely affected were those who had goods on display and multiple bags, boxes and barrels containing goods.

Martina moved along with or more accurately was swept along with the crowd. She held her two bags tightly as the tides swept her along and lodged her at the edge of a fountain, a fenced off section of the park. Another woman was leaning against her, almost pushing her over the fence. She fought to extricate herself but this was difficult as she was holding the bags in her hands. She felt a hand as if it were bracing her off the fence. She didn't know whether this was good or bad and she flipped around like a wind whipped sign to find the man with stretched skin who always seemed to be wherever she went, whether he was sitting across the street from her or leaning on a building close by. He was actually holding on to her as if trying to prevent her from falling.

Martina turned and thanked him and he moved away without acknowledging her gratitude. She shrugged her shoulders resignedly and turned her attention to the scene in front of her. From where she stood, she could see what appeared to be a man writhing on the ground. He was groaning loudly and as she watched, a few people rushed towards him. They tried to lift him up and he started screaming like a train whistle. The beasts stopped their round-up of goods and looked at what was happening without going forward to help. This infuriated the crowd which had gathered and they hurled abuse and bottles at the men.

"Imagine yuh treat us like dog, a run we off the street when all we a try do is prevent we pickney dem from turn tief an' starve in dis country!" an irate woman screamed at them.

"Yes we don't want dem turn tief like some a yuh cause when yuh tek the goods some a yuh sell it an' tek the money fi yuhself. Yuh a break di law worse than wi!" a man added, shaking his fist at them and giving them such a dirty look that if looks could kill they would have died immediately.

"Yes yuh a beast from hell look how yuh cause the man to get injury an' yuh don't even try fi help him! Yuh not a human being yuh a animal being; woman a not yuh mother, a animal yuh come from!" The speaker was advancing towards them with a long umbrella in his hand.

"If yuh come closer a going to put yuh in the jeep along with the goods then yuh really going to see the animal in us!" The metro officer stood his ground, his words and looks pinning the man in mid-stride.

"Yuh a wicked, yuh a tief, a box bread outa poor people mouth!" a woman screamed from the safety of the back of the crowd.

The persons who had rushed to help the fallen man had stopped a taxi and were trying to put him in when there was a loud noise accompanied by a hail of missiles; juice boxes, bottles, stones, anything that was at hand.

"Woi Jesus a wah dis!" one of the officers shouted. "Try

don't let one a dem catch mi or else!"

His words were followed by more missiles. They were coming hard and fast and the men started running in all directions covering their heads, ducking and hiding behind any available shelter. The persons putting the injured man into the taxi also ran for cover, dropping the man on the ground. Everything became chaotic and in the confusion some people started stoning one another instead of the officers. It was the police that quelled the pandemonium. They swooped down like hawks, sirens blaring and screaming, scattering the crowd which had taken advantage of the confusion to snatch back what they could of the goods. When they screeched to a hasty halt, the only evidence of the bedlam was scattered goods and the officers emerging warily from their hiding places.

Martina went back to the location she had been at the first week. She didn't see Tattoo Dye, but Display Board was still there and so were others whom she had not seen before. She nodded her greetings to her and leaned on the wall, praying for her goods to be finished and the day to end so that she could leave that place. She didn't necessarily want to go home but where else could she go?

Two hours later, her bags much lighter, she decided to leave. As she made her way towards the bus stop, she was approached by two young men in their early twenties. They flanked her, forcing her to stop. She looked from one to the other. They looked like brigands with their scarred faces, cornrows and unkempt natural hair, jeans dropped below their bottoms and smelling strongly of ganja. Martina felt her heart slump into her shoes and she shivered involuntarily. At the same time the inevitable question jumped into her mind, what did they want? If they wanted the day's money she would gladly hand it over rather than get into an argument with them. They looked like the type that would not hesitate to inflict scars like the ones on their faces to anyone who crossed them. Evil shone from the devilish glint in their eyes.

"My girl yuh been selling here for three weeks now an' is time yuh pay up some protection money!" Cornrow said without preamble and without looking directly at Martina.

"Well, a didn't know anything bout that," Martina managed to stutter, resuming walking and not looking at the men.

"Well now yuh know," Cornrow said. "Is five hundred dollars a week. One of us will collect every week on a Wednesday morning. Today is Wednesday, an' yuh will get one week free so the fee is one grand." He said it in a matter of fact way as if they had a previous agreement and he had come to settle it. Martina was flabbergasted! Some words rushed to her mouth, but prudence prevailed and she quickly handed over the money she had made for the day. She watched nervously as the extortionists counted out the thousand dollars and handed her back the change. They walked off without a backward glance, having carried out their assignment.

Martina watched them go with sadness pressing down on the inside. She would much prefer to give every single cent to the poor and dispossessed rather than healthy young men who did not want to work but enjoyed reaping the fruits of other people's labour. After she had been punished by the sun, almost trampled by the vendors and spent so much of her precious time amassing the few dollars, she had to hand it over just like that, without a fight, without a word! She was really losing her spunk by just giving in to hoodlums. The anger rose within her. She felt the blood surging upward in her body and felt as if it would flow through her nostrils and choke her. So that was how the town was organised because she felt the young men were working for someone bigger. Well, it would be long but not forever, Martina told herself as she sat wearily in the bus. Dejection weighed heavily on her body and shut out the chatter of the people, the sound of the traffic and the dreams she had cherished of working and saving enough for university.

Miss Turner did not fail to notice her dejection as she came in and slumped down into a chair, the weight of the world weighing heavily in her demeanour, this must have been how the legendary Atlas felt with his daily interminable task.

"Tina girl yuh look drain, you look more than tired! Dat job yuh doing must be very hard! Yuh leave early a morning an' come in late evening, a really sorry a so it turn out," Miss Tuner commented, hobbling over to her. She hugged Martina and she felt that at least somebody cared enough to want to comfort her. She could not disclose any of what had happened to her, nor the details of her 'job' so she simply hugged her back.

"You can say that again Miss Turner, the work really hard fi true, if it wasn't that a really need the money a would give it up." She sighed heavily, the burden of her deception adding to her dejection.

"Well girl, is only a pity dat I too old to help out! A feel like a burden on yuh. Yuh are young an' should be enjoying your young days an' following yuh dream, but instead you have to be working so hard." She sat next to Martina and the helplessness escaped in her sigh.

"Miss Turner, at your age you should be doing exactly what you are doing, sitting, relaxing and enjoying life! My only regret is that you are not enjoying it as you should because of the limited funds and the cramped space." She hugged Miss Tuner again.

"A glad yuh come home cause Yvette doing nothing but sulking an' ignoring me when a talk to her, is like she lose her manners an' her mind all at once. She a run-down big woman an' she don't know that it will come in time an' then she going to wish she was a girl again."

The concern and sadness in Miss Turner's voice were hard to listen to. Martina knew that her help and advice had been invaluable and she was the only mother they knew. She decided to talk to Yvette after she had some rest and had reconciled herself to what had happened that day. The anger had not yet subsided and she didn't want to release it on Yvette and make things worse.

She sat at the table bemoaning how hapless she was.

Why couldn't it have been the other way around? She got up and put away her bags quietly and then threw her handbag on the table, the straps splayed out on either side of the bag like Anancy in repose. She put her head down on the table and her tiredness induced sleep relieved her from the unpleasant thoughts that were the story of her life. Miss Turner came back into the room and woke her telling her to go and lie down but she murmured something unintelligible and went back to sleep.

She woke with a start and for a while she did not know where she was or understand what was happening and then she heard the shots slamming into the concrete. Pow! Pow! Pow! Bap! Bap! Bap! She dived under the table and covered her ears as if that could cover and protect her. She was sure it was her house and she wondered where Miss Turner and Yvette were and if they were all right, but she could not shout out or crawl around while the shooting was going on.

She removed her hands from her ears and the shooting was still going on. The shooters certainly wanted to rain all the shots they had into the building and the people inside.

The shooting went on for more than a minute and Martina cringed in untold fear, imagining every evil, Miss Turner dead, Yvette dead and anybody else who was nearby. What could have sparked the shooting? Did it have anything to do with the man who had threatened her or had the young men followed her from work? She did not know what to think. One thing she knew was that she would not surface from under the table until she was sure the shooter or shooters were gone and she heard the voices of the people she knew would gather to investigate, comment and help if needs be.

"Jesus Christ, a wonder if dem alive in there?" came the first voice.

"No sah, they mus' dead is over twenty shot mi count an' dem mus' connect somebody!"

"But Jesus a why dem shoot up the house after no criminal no live right here soh!" The voice was incredulous, questioning.

Another one shouted, "Shim! Shim! Boss! My yute! Answer if yuh living an' shut up if yuh dead!"

Martina sprung from under the table as if she were a shot propelled from a gun. She dashed inside the room and shouted out Yvette and Miss Turner's names.

"Yvette! Miss Turner! Jesus, yuh alive? Weh yuh deh?" Panic took over her voice as she ran into the room. "Weh yuh deh?" She screamed out when she saw no one. "Yvette! Miss Turner, you hurt or dead? Answer me!"

"Tina, Tina, take it easy, take it easy," Miss Turner answered in a muffled, subdued voice which came from under the bed. She pushed out her head and Martina ran towards her.

"Where is Yvette?" she asked, anxiously peering under the bed as she reached forward to pull Miss Turner out.

"I'm all right." Yvette's voice came, low and unwilling.

"Thank God a wonder if Shim and his family alright? It sound like is over his house that really get shoot up. A going out to check. Remember don't say or do anything that will cause people to find out the relationship between us." She said the last in a cautionary tone looking from one to the other. Yvette did not look frightened, she just continued wearing the sullen look which had become part of her demeanour. Martina felt a pain in her heart but decided not to say anything to her just yet.

She opened the door gingerly and peered out at the sight of the huge crowd. She decided not to ask herself where the people had come from so quickly. It was the norm in crowded living and working areas for a huge crowd to materialize in mere minutes and Port-Herb was no exception. Moreover, shooting was involved and that magnetic force always galvanized people to gather.

She merged with the crowd at the same time trying to get close to Shimron so she could see his condition and hear his story.

He saw her but gave no indication that he had, and then he repeated information which she was certain was for her benefit because he must have said that already to the questioning crowd.

"As a open the door an' step inside the man dem jus' open up like sudden thunder! All a could do was hit the ground like ripe breadfruit an' then crawl in the corner!" Despite the dramatic story, his face was impassive and drawn and his eyes dead. After he spoke he just stood and listened to the comments and noise around him.

"My God! Jah know star, a count bout twenty-five bullet

hole in the house!" one man shouted out to the crowd.

"From when no rain don't fall but it rain bullet pan dis house tonight!" another man remarked.

"My yute yuh lucky de house save you this time, but yuh know that dem coming back for yuh!" another shouted from the back of the crowd.

One lady who had apparently gone to bed and had run out in her nightie shouted, "My yute a really what yuh do or mix up inna?"

Her question started a mumbling in the crowd, Martina overheard scamming and gang involvement. Martina was not a committed Christian but she believed in God and his mercy and did not see Shimron's escape as being fortuitous. It was divine intervention, a warning from God to leave the area. She just felt that the motive was his refusal to join the gang. Her surmising was interrupted by the whining and wailing of a police siren. Martina welcomed their presence; at least some semblance of order and a slight restoration of hope would attain.

The crowd parted like the waters of the Red Sea, allowing unimpeded passage for three officers who bore sombre, solemn looks on their faces. The others stayed at the back of the crowd.

"Who lives in this house?" one of them questioned.

Two of the officers took Shimron inside, while the others at the back moved up to examine the house as a second vehicle bearing more officers swooped down.

When Shimron opened the door for the officer, Martina

caught a glimpse of a tearful Nadra holding the baby. She was happy that they were alright. She went back inside and sat down, she would call Shimron later and talk to him.

Eight

It was two weeks after the incident with Shimron and Martina was still reeling from what had happened. Walking around downtown and trying to sell while looking out for the extortionists was taking a toll on her nerves. She was not a weakling but her life was spiralling downwards in terms of achieving her dreams and she was becoming disillusioned. No mother, no father, separated from her brother, estranged from her sister, she felt really lonely. The same night of the incident Shimron had been whisked away by the police officer who had helped him when he had been shot a few years before. He had telephoned him and told him what had happened and true to his promise that he would always be there for him, he allowed him to stay at his house for a week and then he found a place and had arranged for his furniture to be transported. Martina felt as if a part of her had been torn out but she could not allow anyone outside to see the tears and the pain. She had spoken to him almost every day and he had confessed to her that he knew she was selling downtown. Somebody had seen her and told him and even though he did not want her to, he told her to continue until he had found a job for her.

She felt a little relieved that he had found out and thought she was very brave and humble about the whole thing. He warned her about the dangers and promised he would visit her when things had settled down and he could arrange a secret meeting.

Martina was lost thinking about her problem and did not see the two little boys until one touched her foot. She jumped aside and then looked down and it was then that she saw them, two little boys approximately eight and six years old, sitting by the side of the street looking hungry and confused. The one who had touched her stretched out his hand to her, palm upwards beseeching for food.

"Miss beg yuh a bag juice please."

"An' me too, beg yuh a juice please."

Martina looked at them and sympathy pulled at her heart. It was plain that they were related; they had the same long egg-shaped face with huge brown eyes tormented and haunted by hunger. Their faces and hands were stained with dirt and she could see the malnourishment sticking out of their meagre frames. She could tell that they were weak as they could hardly stand. She quickly gave them two juices each and two bags of banana chips. She was so saddened by their plight that she would do anything to help them. Here were two children who seemed worse off than she was and immediately she remembered the age-old story of the banana skin. Generations of people had told the story of a man who was so poor and disillusioned by life that he decided to commit suicide. He had only a ripe banana to eat and he climbed a tree to jump to his death but ate the banana first and then threw the skin to the ground. When he looked down another human being had picked up the skin and was eating it. He was shocked by the realization that there was someone who was worse off than he was so he got down out of the tree and decided to try again. It was Miss Turner who had told Martina and Yvette the story, encouraging them not to think they were the worst. Selling downtown had made Martina realize this more and more every day. It had provided a little flicker of hope to know that in her penury, she was able to help somebody.

They ate ravenously, apparently the meagre fare she had supplied was to them a great feast. She tried to find out more about them as they ate. "What is your name?"

The younger of the two swallowed slowly and answered shortly, unhappy at being disturbed in his eating. "Conrad."

"And you big brother, what is your name?" she asked, watching his mouth as he savoured the food.

"Gunnard but mi mother call mi Gunman cause she say is dat mi going to do." He obviously did not think anything of it because he went back to eating without a change of expression on his face.

Good lord! Martina thought, what kind of mother

would give her child a name like that and then turn around and call him a gunman? "What is your mother's name, Nard?" She refused to use the first part of his name, it was too outrageous! She wished there was a law against people punishing their children with their mistakes by inflicting them with stupid names and speaking evil into their lives with their very words.

"Miss Ma'am," volunteered the younger boy.

"Miss Ma'am?" Martina was shocked. "That is her little yard name but what is her real name?"

"Yuh soun' like de teacha at de school a use to go," Gunnard commented, looking at Martina as if he were seeing her for the first time.

"No I am not a teacher but a need to find out something about you. Where is your mother and where does she live?" Martina hoped she would get to the bottom of the problem and find out why the little boys were on the street by themselves.

"She gone a country wid de odda four little one. She seh she can't manage de six of us so we mus' beg people food an' clothes an' hope that smaddy will help us." This time it was Conrad who told the story.

Martina was so taken aback that she just stood there looking foolishly at the boys. How could a mother so callously abandon her children? She knew about the young women with the many children for the many fathers who could not be found, or who did not maintain their children. If some of her mother's children had not died she would have been in a similar situation but thank God for divine intervention.

"So where you use to live?" She continued trying to gather more information.

"Down a Big Yaad," Gunnard supplied reluctantly. "Whole heap a wi use to live a Big Yaad."

"But where is Big Yaad?" Martina asked curiously. "Which street?"

"It jus' name Big Yaad. Is a street dat everybody know cause everybody come dere. Whole heap a house an' shop is dere."

Martina knew that setting only too well, it could be any street in any of the inner city communities. A plan formed in her head. She needed to see a police officer and hand over the children because she could not leave them on the street alone.

"Stand right here and don't move, a coming right back," Martina instructed. She had seen a police foot patrol across the road and she wanted to talk to them before they moved away. She didn't know exactly how she would put it but she had to get help for the abandoned children.

"Officer Sir," she started as soon as she was within earshot of the officers. "There's a problem across the road. A mean there are two little boys who have been abandoned by their mother. They are sitting right over there; they need help." The words came tumbling out in a great rush as if they were being pushed by an unseen force.

The officers turned around and looked at the earnest face of the young girl making the report. There was concern and sympathy written in the eyes; she made it sound like an emergency.

"Miss almost every day children are abandoned by their parents; sometimes we can do nothing about it," the older of the two replied in an offhand, dismissive manner.

"Do you know them?" the other asked, scrutinizing her as if she were the offender. His piercing black eyes bored into her in an uncomfortable, disconcerting manner.

"No, if I did, I would try to find their parents and take them back home," Martina fired back, matching his stare. "They can't stay there like that, they have to be placed in state care."

The two officers were now looking at her as if she had spoken for the first time. Her tone and constant use of standard English had caught their attention.

"What you doing down here selling? You don't look or sound like a downtown person," the older policeman said.

"Yes and no. I am a downtown person but that is not the point. The point is the children." She did not like to argue with older people especially police officers, all she wanted to do was to get the children to a place of safety.

The older officer went on his cell phone and called somebody and about half an hour later a vehicle arrived and took the children away. The younger officer gave her a number and told her to call him later in the night but Martina ignored it, promising herself to avoid him if she ever saw him again. She wondered how much of her time she would have to spend evading people.

When she got home that evening Martina got a call from Shimron. He told her that she should meet a man at the stoplight on Orange Street. He described him and the vehicle he drove. Martina would have preferred an interview in an office but trusted Shimron to try and do the best for her. She felt hopeful in getting off the street and getting a normal job for which she was qualified. She could hardly sleep that night.

In the morning, she wore a casually elegant ensemble but carried her usual street outfit so that she could continue her enterprise after the interview. She did not want to seem too anxious so she walked around and did some business and appeared close to the stoplight at exactly nine.

In no fewer than five minutes, Mr. Bentley arrived. He was about forty years old with a hairline which had started to disagree with his forehead and had started to hold it slightly at bay. He had a cultured look about him, which complemented his upright bearing and athletic physique, but his eyes had an undefined quality about them. They gave Martina an idea of an unassuming person who was not really what he seemed to be or perhaps it was her inbuilt mistrust of the male species that was clicking in. The appraising look he gave her did not miss Martina.

"Good morning, you must be Martina," he greeted her. "Your brother did not tell me how attractive and intelligent you look," he continued, motioning towards his black Mercedes Benz.

Martina took one look at the vehicle and recoiled; after her near miss with Dragon no way would she get into a motor vehicle alone with a total stranger, Shimron's boss or not, job or no job, cultured personality or not!

"No sir, I will be quite comfortable standing on the sidewalk or under the shop's roof," she said politely.

"All right, as you wish," he replied, "wherever you are more comfortable."

Martina led the way to a nearby shop piazza where there was a constant flow of people. "Can I call you Martina?" he opened the interview.

"Yes you can sir," Martina replied.

"No don't call me sir, you make me feel ancient." A half smile appeared on Mr. Bentley's face. "The name is Tariff."

In her mind Martina thought of taxes; how did he hope to collect taxes from her?

"Okay, Tariff it is," she said.

"How old are you and what are your qualifications?" He continued looking keenly at her.

"I am eighteen and I have nine CXC all ones and ten units of CAPE, seven ones and three twos. I–"

"What, your brother said you were bright but I had no idea he was talking about pure brilliance! With your personable personality and your brilliance what are you doing selling on the streets of downtown Kingston instead of being in university?" Amazement escaped from his placid countenance.

"Well, I had some family problems, did not get to apply for the students' loan on time and", bitterness crept into her voice, "because of my ghetto connection nobody wants to hire me, so I am trying to work and put a little aside and then borrow students' loan for September."

"You do not have to go through that." Mr. Bentley's voice was low and cool.

"What do you mean?" questioned Martina, looking closely at him.

"Well you can go to university without paying a cent out of your pocket…"

"Oh you mean you could point me to scholarships and bursaries," she chipped in, hope bringing excitement to her voice.

Mr. Bentley looked at her and shook his head. "You do not need to do that. You can go to university free if you are smart." He emphasized 'smart' as his eyes raked her face.

Martina looked at him puzzled. "How is that possible? University is an expensive affair, only the privileged seem able to attend without much financial burden. I am most certainly not in that category so how can it be free?"

"Well…" Mr. Bentley cleared his throat and Martina took that as a sign of hesitancy or searching for the words. "Well, I know someone who would finance you. It is very simple. He would set you up in an apartment and pay your fees, all you have to do is to be there whenever he chooses to visit, no clothes to wash or iron or chores to do except take care of the apartment which would be in a middle-class community and help out one or two of his friends now and again." A wily look crept into his eyes, he was a fox slinking in for the kill of an innocent prey.

Martina felt the ire igniting inside her. Had she not been

taught good manners she would have spat right in his face and deservedly so. For an inner city girl with very little prospect, the offer was tempting, but that kind of offer was for a prostitute or a kept woman. She looked Mr. Bentley squarely in his eyes and with asperity she levelled him. "I should just respond to you with the level of civility that a vermin like you deserve but I will not wallow in the gutter with you! Do you think that all women who live in the ghetto are promiscuous or prostitutes? Do you think that because we sell on the street we are all dogs like you? Did my brother tell you that I was less than an ambitious woman? You, you, you–" the words were glued to her tongue and refused to come out.

"My girl, you know how many young girls make it through life, university and otherwise with that kind of arrangement? What you pretending about? You should be glad that anybody even see you, a ghetto you come from!" Disbelief and anger had eroded the calm, cultured composure. He now looked at Martina as a dish cloth whom he had wanted to make into a tablecloth.

"I am not yet a Christian but I am going to pray for your soul and a hope that poetic justice will reach you! I also hope that God will have mercy on your children because anything you do to others it will come back full circle!" Passers-by were slowing down and looking at them curiously, but Martina did not care. She flounced away leaving him looking after her like a cat who had allowed a lizard to crawl away from it, robbing it of its main meal.

She changed back into her work garb before calling Shimron. This was to allow some of the fury to seep out of her system, but it did not work.

"Shimron how comes you always bawling bout not having money when you mus' be rotten rich, how much you make when you pimp out the girls?" Martina lashed out in condemnation over the phone.

"Tina, but gal yuh get mad or what, who yuh calling pimp?" Iron had struck iron and sparks were flying.

"But you mus' be a pimp cause you send the big man you working with to offer me prostitution job! I did tell you dat mi want turn no lady of the night? You see what happen to mummy? You think a want dat life for myself?"

Shimron had to speedily ease the phone from his ears or his eardrum would have been permanently damaged. He had never heard his sister speak so angrily before. "Tina, Tina, gal, yuh lucky yuh deh so far cause a would really forget myself an' box yuh! Box yuh freshness right down yuh throat! All a do was tell the man dat yuh bright an' dat yuh need a job an' him say aright. Who yuh a call pimp? Wait till a see yuh an' yuh will find out say yuh a push mi right back into badness! Jus'—"

Martina hung up the phone with a snort. What did he think he could do to her? She had no intention of allowing two things to happen to her; one, to be dependent on and be beaten by any man; two, to live the life her mother had lived. She preferred to remain poor and penniless than to have people hold her in derision as they had done her mother when she died. If Shimron wanted to hit her then he knew he would have a fight on his hands! She knew she had been rude but the man had approached with such surety that she could not help thinking he must have been coached.

It did not make her feel any better and she was truly exacerbated when she remembered that she had to pay the extortion fee. Maybe I should have submitted to that pervert she thought irrationally, then I would not have to be subjected to highway robbery! She thought the devil was really out to get her when the regular extortionists did not turn up, but two others claiming they had been sent by Scar Beard and his friend. She handed over her hard-earned cash and went home exasperated, praying for every evil in the world to befall all men who took advantage of females in any way.

Miss Turner offered her comfort when she told her about Mr. Bentley and the falling out with Shimron.

"Tina a know it really hard to see yuh dream within reach an' not being able to achieve it, but guess what, yuh young, yuh have ambition, yuh have time, don't let any man get yuh into any corner an' make you less than a woman. Don't let them use yuh to gratify themself an' guess what, a know of more than one case where young girl wanting to come to something give in to these sugar daddy, yeah man sweet mouth, full a money, could be they father; an' they end up in a kind a prison. They can't go out as they like, can't talk to anybody, is just a prison! Some of these men have dem wife an' pickney at home who dem not leaving so no future not really there for these young girl." She paused in her didactic speech and caught her breath before continuing.

"A heard about this girl who fell in love with somebody else her own age after the sugar daddy sent her to university an' when him find out him kill she an' the young man! Yes many story out there for girls like you to learn from. Don't let money an' easy life rob yuh of yuh dignity. A know yuh might be tempted because of your circumstances but don't let down the people who believe in yuh, an' yuh mus' also believe in yourself an' your ideals. Hold up yuh head, better mus' come one day." She touched Martina's hand and looked her in the eyes to make sure she was getting through to her. "Make your father proud wherever him is an' even if him dead, him dead gone with good things in him mind bout you; don't let him down."

She could hardly sleep that night. Foremost in her mind were the accusations and the harsh words she had spoken to Shimron. She did not need further turmoil in her family especially with Yvette's arctic blast; she did not talk to Martina anymore. In the house, her cell phone was her constant companion. Attempts to talk to her always resulted in rude comments and cold stares as if she were being addressed by an alien or an enemy. Martina had decided to pray and leave her to get the venom out of her system.

She had never really quarrelled with Shimron before, not even when their mother was alive. He was the only male family she had because those on her father's side only seemed to acknowledge her when she was around him. Where were they now? Had they even tried to find out what had happened to Martin's daughter after Aunt Indra had driven her out like a stray dog? She would never know, because even if she had to sleep on the street she would never try to get help from them again! The inner city girl had no place in their uptown life.

Now Shimron was her brother and she needed his support. He was no longer next door and now he had threatened to beat her up. Why had she allowed her anger to rule? But, she chided herself, Shimron might have given the impression that she was easy and desperate. Some men had weird perceptions of women and their needs.

She called him, but after two rings the call was terminated abruptly and thereafter it went straight to voicemail. He was irate and so was she, but nobody could say she hadn't tried to douse the flames.

Nine

It was another sweltering day downtown. Martina pulled her cap down to rescue her face from the onslaught of the pitiless sun. It was only eleven o'clock and the enraged sun had made its presence felt by moulding her wet blouse to her skin. All around her Martina could hear comments about the sun's fury. Display Board had mounted a huge multi-coloured umbrella to protect herself from the attacking sun. She had told Martina that she could stand underneath it to 'cool off' at intervals when she made her rounds and came around to her.

She went and stood underneath the umbrella while Display Board engaged a potential customer. She wished she had somewhere to sit, but failing that she squatted on her haunches and watched the sun's dazzling haze dancing mockingly in front of her. Across the street she could see Taut Face sitting on the sidewalk. She had not seen him for a few days and had wondered if he was frequenting another part of town or had seen better days and had moved on.

People were going about their business as usual and Martina got lost in a maze of thoughts about what was happening to and around her.

She was jerked out of her reverie when a man stormed across the street in her direction followed by a mob with stones and pieces of board in evidence. The vehicles halted momentarily as they streaked across as if they owned the road and had every right to rush across whether there was traffic or not. The impatient blasting and honking of horns did nothing to stop the mob.

As the horde hit the sidewalk, vendors began to swear and grab for machetes because people were bumping into their goods and some of it lay strewn and trampled on the ground. Martina got up swiftly and got out of harm's way as the rabble surged past her. In a fleeting moment, she saw a man and heard his belaboured breathing. She also caught a glint of the knife he bore in his hand. That was not all, even though he was running, Martina caught a glimpse of his face and became immobilized! It was the same man! Even in her deepest sleep she would remember the serious leering eyes, the cornrows and the shirt with the dragon emblazoned on the back. She would always remember the long drive into the country and the heavy wooded area. The gripping fear and the rough, cold touch of his hands were indelibly inscribed in her mind and so too was the glittering glint of the knife which had kept her captive while she wished for a swift death instead of the double torture of being raped and killed. The voice was still ripping in her ears, 'Nobody, an' a mean nobody, escape from Dragon'. The nightmares she had experienced all came rushing like the wind to her mind, causing more sweat to pour from her body and her blouse to become one with her skin.

She was dragged from her flashback by the words, "Him a rapist him fi dead! Many girls him rape! Long run short ketch! Every day bucket go a well one day di bottom mus' drop out! Dutty pervert, let wi string him up!"

Martina was jerked back to reality and despite her resolve never to join crowds or run in the direction of fights and gunshots, she decided to run after the mob. She just had to see what would become of this danger to society and get the full story of how he had been caught. She held her bags tightly and waited until the mob had passed and then tore after them, bringing up the rear. Behind her she could hear police sirens, an unwelcome sound to the people who did not just want to hand him over to the police but rather inflict their own form of jungle justice. She did not believe in people taking justice into their own hands or killing people at their own accord. Even though she knew it was wrong she wanted him to suffer as he had caused her and others to suffer even if it was to get a good beating which she would not assist in doing.

The chase ended at the old fountain where he was cornered by some other men. Some of them were themselves wrongdoers, scammers and extortionists or involved in crimes of different sorts but quick to condemn others once a public chance offered itself. How did this salve their consciences? Some of the women too were guilty of prostituting themselves and encouraging their young daughters to get into affairs with older influential men for money, wasn't that a form of rape in itself? Yet here they all were, the good, the bad, the indifferent and the victims, ready for the kill.

When Martina arrived, Dragon was leaning against the old fountain trying to defend himself with his knife. He reminded Martina of a cornered wild boar using his tusks to try and gore his enemies. As he tried to fend off the offenders, people hurled abuses at him.

"All rapist fi dead!"

"A string we going to string you up an' bobbet yuh!"

"A long time we know bout yuh an' want fi catch yuh tail!"

Hurling abuses were not enough so they rained stones, bottles and other missiles at him. One of the stones hit the knife out of his hand and he stood bare and defenceless like a helpless plant caught in the midst of a raging hurricane, being buffeted and beaten by the wind and water.

Martina turned her face away in horror. She had taken care to position herself at the back, yet inside the crowd, so that when the incident went viral, as she knew it would, she would not be caught on camera. That was the last thing she wanted as somebody, somehow, would make the connection between Dragon and herself. She thought he had had enough and that the people should leave the law to take care of the rest.

As she turned away keeping her head down, a gunshot

rang out. At first she was uncertain where it had come from and rushed back to the side of the crowd not wanting to be conspicuous or trampled if there was a stampede.

Somebody in the crowd warned, "Police, Pow, Pow! Police! Pow! Pow!"

The police fired in the air again and the crowd scattered in all directions like seeds being blown by the wind. Martina ran to the back of a stall and stood there, panting and watchful. From her vantage point she saw that the park was empty except for an inert form lying on the concrete. The police stood looking at Dragon and then they looked around but there was no one to talk to as the people had disappeared like chaff blown away by the wind. Two of them lifted Dragon between them and placed him into the jeep.

"Him lucky him still alive," a stall owner observed.

"But how you know dat?" a potential customer questioned.

"Miss if him did dead dem would a put yellow tape round the area an' leave him right there for a long time while dem collect evidence, but see dem put him in the jeep an' turn on the siren so a public hospital dem carry him gone, a so di t'ing set." He beamed with superior knowledge at the ways of the police. Selling downtown for years had given him wisdom.

"But a how di story really go?" asked another woman who had stopped by. Things were now returning to normal.

"As far as me hear, from long time people suspect that a him a rape off the woman dem but him smart an' dem couldn't catch him cause him keep moving around from place to place an' dem

say him deal wid D Lawrence so it did hard fi catch him."
The stall owner stopped in his story and tried to seize an
opportunity to make a sale. "A see you eyeing the jeans dem,
dem on sale out so you can look pan all a dem an' tell mi
which one a dem you like in the meantime."

"But a how dem really get fi chase him like dat?"
another vendor who had worked her way over to the stall
asked. She relaxed and held her bags loosely in her hands,
not wanting to miss the details of the story.

"One a de woman that him fool roun' see him an' give
the alarm an' then another one bawl out that him did rape
her too an' a so it start. Him make a mistake today cause
dem say him always sit in him taxi so him can drive off easy
easy, but today for whatever reason him come out an' lean up
on the taxi an' a so dem see him," the vendor related. Other
people had surrounded the stall, people were always ready
for a good story especially if excitement was in it.

"Yuh remember the school girl from the big shot high
school dat dem did fine in the bush bout two or three years
back? I hear that is him did tek her way an' cause her fi
nearly dead! I don't know how truth it be but a so mi buy it
a so mi sell it," supplied another woman from the growing
numbers around the stall.

"Well whether a so or not mi glad him come off de street,
him give the other taxi man dem bad name, everybody a
look on dem like rapist. A jus' hope the woman dem go
identify him so dat him can dead in prison! I not sorry fi
him! A hope dem don't let him get away!" she repeated

emphatically as if she were talking to the women themselves.

"Well put your mind at rest because Neeta that see him first an' bawl out a go make sure that. An' anyway it better him stay in lock-up cause if him come back out here dog nyam him supper!"

Martina listened to all they had to say and then slinked away like a wild cat. She had heard enough. There were two things she was happy about; the first was that Dragon had been caught, he would no longer hurt any other female, and the second was that she would not have to face the courts and give evidence because she was not the only 'victim' and others would only be too ready to testify against him. Despite her situation she was overjoyed that one of her dreams had come through and as fate would have it, she had been a witness to a part of Dragon's punishment.

She started making her way back to her favourite section where Display Board vended. No matter where she ventured, she always came back to that spot because business was sometimes better there and even though they did not talk much there was this unspoken camaraderie between them. She had not seen Tattoo Dye for a week and learnt he had other businesses to attend to.

She stopped abruptly and her heart did a fast flip. She only had time enough to dodge around two passers-by and hide around the corner. She strained her ears trying to overhear what they were saying to Display Board but, she could not. Her first thought was to take off to another section of town but curiosity held her captive. She wanted to find out how they had found her.

She watched them like a cat watching fish and when they had finished talking and turned to go, she disappeared around the corner and across the street. She would go back before she went home to find out how Andre and Leonie had found her. She figured that somebody had seen her and told them as they were not persons who frequented downtown. Was it that they were really interested in her or was it out of curiosity that they wanted to see her? Well, they would only see her if they came upon her suddenly because in her present state she did not want to see them. A surge of slight envy sprang up as she realized that she could have been enjoying the status of being a university student as well. She would have to change her favourite spot now that she had been discovered, but who had given her away?

She walked around to another street where there seemed to be less human activity. This was not good for business but she would take her chances, there were too many things happening around the other side.

She settled against a tree and took note of what was happening around her. She did not think Andre and Leonie would venture to this section. They would be well on their way to their own world by now. This section was the beauty salon area. There were a number of young ladies involved in weaving, braiding and colouring hair. They had a folding table on which the items were placed and three young women were getting their hair done while a few others waited. As the business went on, they discussed the happenings of the day, the hot topic was Dragon's beating.

"A so sorry a wasn't round dat side cause a would certainly help to beat him!" one of the hairdressers remarked. Her nostrils flared furiously, causing the nose ring she wore to vibrate with emotion.

"The government cause dem to get off too easy so that's why dem will always continue dem evil," responded one of the customers. "If a was around there…"

Her speech was interrupted when a Rastafarian man approached with a young child in his hand. The talker jumped up in panic, upsetting the stool she was sitting on.

"Dread a what, what yuh a do down here?" She could hardly get the words out. She looked ridiculous with half of her hair hanging loose like a coloured wet mop and the other half resembling a chopped off dog's tail.

"Lafta, what me a do down here? From mawning yuh left the house and left the baby with Miss Minnie say you going to buy school things and this is how you buying the books, a put in HBO in your hair. I man vex bout dat!" He shook his fist at her.

"Dread, HBO? After is not movie we a watch! HBO is a movie station." This came from one of the women waiting to get her hair done. Everyone burst into laughter.

"Black woman from Africa, don't act stupid! HBO mean hair borrowed from others. You don't know that?" A quizzical look came into his eyes.

"Is not borrow mi borrow the hair is buy mi buy it!" Lafta

exclaimed, aghast.

"So you use the pickney dem book money and buy people hair fi comb into yours! Empress you mus' know yourself! That hair don't look like synthetic hair so a mus' the Brazilian hair that cost much more money that you have a comb into your hair." He was furious and advanced towards her as he spoke, fury rushing out of his eyes.

"But Dread nothing no wrong wid putting in hair, it cause we to look better and a know you men love to see when we look better." The speaker was one of the women who was having her hair done. "We look real hot."

"Yes you look hot with ignorance. It pain mi heart fi see black woman so fool fool! Did you know that you a put on other people distress on top a you head when you comb in dem so call real hair into you head? Only a woman who have problem would cut off her lovely hair and sell it! You did know that? Some of the woman have mental problem, some a prostitute, some poor an' every other kind a problem. Idiot, only fool take up problem that other people put down! When you comb in HBO you a comb in people problem in your hair!" His eyes were passionate with his revelation, his locks were flopping from side to side to help emphasize his words.

"Dread yuh know a never really think about it dat way. What yuh seh really make whole heap a sense but what yuh don't know won't hurt yuh. We don't know the woman dem whose hair we using so it won't hurt," one of the hair-dressers replied.

"Woman what difference it mek whether you know which woman de hair come from? The t'ing is you a comb people problem into you head. And another t'ing, why the hair that you woman comb into yuh hair have to be so long?" He was clearly becoming incensed with his subject.

"Well long hair look better, that's why we prefer it. It really look better, give yuh hair some body and character," one of the customers defended.

"Woman a not even a call yuh Empress cause that word truly belong to good looking conscious African woman! Woman if Jah did want you to have long hair him would a give you from birth. And the worst part is along with people long hair you colour it blue, green, red, orange every colour of the rainbow and all that Berger dream up and mix! In all my forty odd year on this earth me never see black woman born with any of those colour in dem head, is only black and a kind of brownish colour when some pigment t'ing go wrong." Dread's lips were jumping madly, expressing the extent of his conviction.

"But Lord Dread how yuh so boring, is only to look hot and different why we do it, a nuh anything else!" one of the hairdressers tried to explain lamely.

"No is not only dat black woman have a problem wid themselves. They don't like dem black complexion and dem will do anything to let dem look close to the enslaver. Fire fi di whole a yuh! Lightning and thunder on this evil dat reach Jah nostril!" Dread uttered the words looking up to heaven as if to evoke the lightning and thunder he had spoken about.

"Boy yuh really feel passionate about this hair thing," one of the women observed. "Is the first time mi really hear anybody carry on so bout hair."

"Come tek the baby and let me tell you something woman, don't come into my little two by two with you hair look like flowers garden or else...member mi tell you dat! And make sure dat you present di pickney dem book money as soon as you step through the door!" He handed the baby to the almost tearful Lafta and walked off in a huff without even a backward glance.

"Lord Jesus Laffy what yuh going do now?" her hairdresser asked with a doleful look on her face.

"Me don't even know cause more than half of it comb already." Distress broke in her voice and the baby started to cry.

"Yuh know what let all a wi pull it out. Is a good thing it don't comb too fine," offered one of the women.

Lafta sat on a stool and four of them gathered around and started undoing the style.

"But Lafta, don't say mi fast but yuh did really know that Dread nuh like dem kind a hair business yah?" the hairdresser asked, looking at Lafta in a puzzled manner.

"To tell yuh the truth yes, but mi never really pay him no mind cause a no jus' to look good for him, mi want to feel good about myself too an' mi want to look hot when mi step out. A don't want to look ordinary an' like no church sister." The vexation was evident in her voice.

"Hi mind yourself," one of the women pulling out the hair cautioned. "Nothing no wrong with looking like Christian. Don't you believe in God?" she questioned.

"Yes, a never say a don't believe in God, mi go church w'en mi ready but mi still like the bling an' hotness!"

"Seem to me yuh have to decide whether yuh a stay with Dread or not," the hairdresser commented, beckoning another customer to sit.

Martina had listened to the whole exchange keenly and she found Dread's viewpoint different and interesting. She herself did not really like extensions and hair colouring but at the same time she didn't have a problem with people expressing themselves unless it went overboard like the too long hair or excessive colouring. If as he said black women had a problem with themselves, which she thought they did for other reasons, then it was really something to look into.

She had decided to call it a day and was on her way back to talk to Display Board when two familiar figures appeared like spectres beside her. She was amazed seeing that they had already sent two of their cronies to collect from her. She ignored them and walked faster but Scar Beard stepped in front of her and blocked her path.

"My girl how yuh a move so? Mi get the impression dat yuh trying to avoid us!" He tried to smile but only a snarl appeared.

"How many times in one week yuh coming to collect from mi?" she asked, looking at him bravely, sternly.

"My girl what yuh mean? Yuh see us from week?" He seemed genuinely surprised.

"Two men come and collect already say you send dem!" Sweat started to form in her palms, this could not be happening.

"My girl we don't work wid nobody, nobody! We neva sen' nobody to yuh. Yuh have to pay again an' be careful next time." He held out his hand and Martina reluctantly paid him. He smirked and they walked away. Tears spilled over and she wiped them away fiercely, hastily. She would not let anyone see her crying. She knew she had to make some decisions fast but later for that.

She composed herself, pushing aside the contorted, tormenting thoughts; she had to hear from Display Board what Leonie and Andre wanted. She waited until she had dispensed with her two customers and then she approached her.

"Hi, how things?" she asked to open the conversation.

"Not bad, could be better but give t'anks to de Father. A don't see yuh from yuh follow de crowd, what happen?" Display Board looked at her curiously.

"Oh just wanted to see who the man was. Him get a real good beating!"

"Good fi him, don't like dem kind a man deh. Him lucky de police save him. But what happen, yuh face look sad." She peered anxiously at Martina as if the answer would pop out.

In as few words as possible she told her about the two sets of extortionists.

"What my girl! Tell one a dem to come roun' me an' see if dem don't end up like Dragon! Is cause yuh look young an' simple! Dem prey on de innocent. Why yuh never tell me from de first time?" She hissed her teeth defiantly as if the extortionists were standing right in front of her. "Anyway another t'ing."

Martina tried not to show any interest in what she was going to say even though Display Board could not speak quickly enough for her.

"Girl, two of yuh friend from school show up looking for yuh. A always know there was something different bout yuh, like yuh educated or something but hiding it. Dem say they been trying to get yuh but yuh not answering de phone. Dem begging yuh to call dem or allow dem to come an' talk to yuh, especially de young man. Him seem more than normally concern." She smiled at Martina in a very suggestive way.

Martina looked back at her serious and thoughtful without giving anything away. She felt good that her friends were concerned about her, but she didn't want them to see her as she was now; she didn't want sympathy and pity. Maybe she was too proud or was poor and 'boasty' but she wanted to meet them when she was on their level, a student working to achieve her dreams.

"Yes they are friends, yes a should be where they are but a having some money problems." She stopped there, not wanting to disclose any fine details about her life.

"Well yuh just need fi get somebody to help yuh. A bright girl like yuh deserve a chance in life. Give me yuh number an' take mine too. A going to ask somebody bout a job if a get to see him before him go back a foreign." They exchanged numbers and Martina found it strange that she did it without hesitating and put it down to the fact that she had a liking for Display Board. Even so, she did not want to tell her, her life story.

Ten

s Martina sat on the bus, she watched the clouds at
play. It was almost evening and in addition to nature
pulling down its cover over the day to signal time off
from work, the clouds were making their presence felt. They
had completely obscured the waning sun with frowning blackness
and seemed to have moved closer to earth in a threatening
bid. The few straggling white clouds quickly got out of their
way and those which failed to do so were overrun by the black
clouds which formed indistinct shapes of mountains and huge
puffs of smoke. To add more menace to their demeanour, the
lightning streaked across the sky renting the blackness, and the
thunder not to be outdone, bellowed a sudden ominous warning.

Martina hoped she could get home before the rain, she did
not like sheltering on the road, especially at the piazzas with
the men making suggestive jokes. She was certainly not in the
mood for anti-social men blowing pungent ganja and
cigarette smoke into her nostrils, choking and infecting her
lungs.

Once she got off the bus she walked fast and half-ran down the street chased by the drops of rain which were increasing in size and volume as she ran. Opening an umbrella would be a futile exercise as the wind would tear it from her hand and bear it away.

She opened the door as the deluge started, glad that she had not been thoroughly soaked. Miss Turner met her at the door and closed it quickly, proffering a large towel at the same time.

"Girl yuh lucky, yuh almost get wash away," she joked, greeting Martina. "Yuh luckier than Yvette, I don't see her from evening, plus see the rain come and catch her out."

"But school give holiday from yesterday so why she gone out and I don't think she get any summer job," Martina remarked, removing her wet shoes.

"When a wake up I didn't see her cause a went back to bed after yuh leave an' over-sleep. I didn't wake up till 8:30," said Miss Turner.

"Well a hope she not gone far and a hope she don't bring any more trouble into this family cause the way she behaving a not too certain what she up to." Martina's eyes had an unsettled look, she didn't quite know what to make of Yvette's intractable behaviour, right now she just wanted to curl up in her bed and enjoy the rain before dealing with some decisions she had to make.

She folded up herself like a blind person's walking stick and slept with the rain drumming euphoniously on the slab roof. It lulled her into a false sense of complacency, intoxicating and heady. She didn't even dream about any of her pressing problems, this drug just kept her under its soothing influence. Alas, this was short-lived, the rain ceased after an hour and its cessation jolted her back to reality.

She sat up suddenly in the bed and yawned noisily. Why had the rain stopped, she questioned inwardly. It had been such a balm to a troubled mind. She showered slowly as if the water was an extension of the rain and could offer delaying tactics.

Afterwards she sat in the room quietly, not wanting to wake Miss Turner. She turned on the television and listened to the news. There was the perpetual crime problem which sometimes prevented her from watching the news, it was just too much. She watched it half-heartedly, wanting to block out the gory details. She sat up suddenly as the presenter started a special report on human trafficking. In this his first report, his focus was on different types of human trafficking and how it was made possible. He said that human trafficking was the trade of humans, most commonly for the purpose of sexual slavery, forced labour, or commercial sexual exploitation for the trafficker or others. He also pointed out that millions were trafficked across the world annually, 80% of which were females and half of that percentage, children. It was pointed out that billions were made from sex trafficking. These traffickers often targeted victims and overcame them by coercion, lies, threats and violence. On the whole, the report was educational and informative and Martina looked forward to hearing the other sections, especially the interviews with survivors.

At the end of the news a number of missing persons were posted and Martina almost fell off her chair when she saw Stone Cold being featured as one of the missing. Now she must be a neophyte she thought, because in her mind only lower-class girls or women in unfortunate situations went missing! Stone Cold was 'white' and from the upper class. Young women like that did not go missing. She felt she had to investigate the circumstances of her disappearance when she had time. Stone Cold was her high school tormentor, but that did not make her feel good about her disappearance.

She shifted her mind to her challenges and the first one was Yvette. Now where had she been all day? It was almost 9 o'clock and she was not in. She had spoken to her sullen frame the day after Shimron's house had been shot up. She had used the incident to concretize the importance of being indoors after dusk especially if one had no good reason to be outside. She acquiesced by nodding a reluctant yes and Martina felt she fully understood what she was saying; so, where was she? The rain had ceased for quite a while now so she should have made her way home.

She turned her mind to her business venture. Her secret had been revealed to her friends and she wished she had the perspicacity to know the way forward. Would Cross Roads be a better place since it was less frequented by people or should she start job hunting again, work for four days and job hunt for two days? She had to make up her mind by the weekend. In her indecisiveness, she dialled her father's number but got no response. She couldn't discuss it with Miss Turner because she did not want to confess that she had lied about her job.

At this point Miss Turner came into the living room and sat down opposite Martina. The worry and fear in her eyes pulled at Martina's heart.

"Unless she in the bathroom, which I feel she is not, I tek it Yvette not home yet." Miss Turner's voice got lower and lower as she made the observation.

"This is the second time she is doing this and I don't know why! A feel she somehow want to punish us, make us suffer because we care too much." Martina was on the verge of tears. She blinked them back because she did not like being a 'cry-baby'. Girls in her situation could not afford to cry over everything, they had to be like stones, be able to weather the elements at all times and not break.

A knock on the door invaded her thoughts and she froze. Well, she reasoned, Yvette was home and she didn't know what she would say to her but she was glad she was home. Both Miss Turner and herself went to the door and as was customary they peeped through a little hole in the door before opening it. Martina peeped first like a rat peeping out for the cat. She drew away fast and placed her finger on her lips and then beckoned to Miss Turner. Miss Turner interpreted the non-verbal signal and then followed her.

"It's not Yvette," whispered Martina, "two men standing out there." Her eyes reflected the fear she was feeling inside.

Had they come to give bad news about Yvette?

"Do not open the door!" Miss Turner warned. "Whatever they want to say let dem say it through the window because we don't know dem an' what dem up to!"

Martina nodded in agreement and went to the door when the knock came again. "Who is it?" she asked.

"Open up and you will see!" a coarse, threatening voice ordered impatiently.

"Nobody who live down here don't open their door to anybody at night, so who you and what you want?" Martina was trying to be brave, but her heart was knocking against her chest so hard that it was in danger of escaping.

"Look here gal don't play!" the hoarse voice answered. "A don't have time to waste!" He knocked on the door again, a loud whack which might have damaged it somehow.

"Well a not opening my door at this time of night so tell mi what you want." Miss Turner had decided to take them on. Her voice was tremulous, yet firm.

"You a hear mi gal Tina or whatever you name. Big Man Tornado seh you mus' come by him house no later than tomorrow night." His voice was definitive, final.

"Who is Big Man Tornado and what would I want at his yard?" Martina clutched the window for support, she could not be hearing right.

"How you mean who name Big Man Tornado? Everybody in Port-Herb know Tornado an' know that yuh nuh joke wid him! If him call yuh him call yuh an' don't second guess cause if yuh don't go him going to get yuh same way, so nuh bother hitch!" The voice was now low and threatening.

"Gal yuh hear, nuh bother hitch!" said a new voice, concretizing the command.

"A have no business with Big Man Tornado so I don't know why him would want to see me," Martina flung back.

"Well a not standing out here all night. A stand up too long a ready. Jus' remember dat Ringo an' Tom Tom deliver de message an' try reach there or else the t'ree a yuh ago pay!" He shouted the last warning as if Martina had grown deaf in one ear.

She heard them moving away and both Miss Turner and herself were transfixed to the spot like they had been turned into blocks of wood.

Miss Turner was the first to speak. "Lawd Jesus Tina it did come to mi mind from long time dat something like this would happen." The tears spilled down her cheeks like water running out of control from a tap which had been turned out too much.

Martina's eyes and nose were pricking and burning with tears but she pushed them back forcefully, she was not going to cry. "Miss Turner," she whispered, holding her hand and pulling her into the bathroom. She turned on the shower lightly and whispered as loudly as she could because she was not sure if the men were gone. They might have pretended to do so and then doubled back.

"A have a plan, for I would rather die than surrender myself to that man whoever he is!" The will to fight forced its way into her voice; this was the old Martina who had taken on Stone Cold when the burden was too much. She was going to find a way out just like when Dragon wanted to have his way with her. She whispered to Miss Turner feverishly for a while and then put her finger over her lips like she was being forbidden to talk at basic school.

She went back to the door in the living room and peeped out but saw no one. She also peeped through the window but they were not there. She sat down and turned on the television, telling herself that determination and persistent effort would strengthen her and help her to fight the enemy of fear and perverted behaviours. She had heard about Big Man Tornado, he was not really the don but he was thought of highly because of his affluence. He did not live in the area but did business there and had many people working for him and also many women who had children for him. He choose young ambitious women who were not involved in relationships because they wanted to make something of their lives. It was rumoured that he had fathered over thirty children. Martina had decided that she would not be giving him the next child even if she had to die trying. The messengers said she had until the next night so right now she would turn her attention to Yvette who still had not turned up.

She called her cell phone several times but it went straight to voicemail. What game was Yvette playing? Martina got up and paced the floor, back and forth, back and forth like the pendulum of a clock. She twisted her fingers, prayed and peeped through the window; no Yvette. A pain started at the back of her head, steady and throbbing at times, then with frequent spasms which spread all over her head. She sat down and rested her head on the table. A slight groan escaped from her and then she started a concentrated battle, fighting back the tears which were adamant that they wanted to make themselves visible. Martina battled them and won and fell into a fitful sleep. She dreamt she was searching for Yvette but when she found her, she ran away laughing, taunting her to follow her.

"Come Reada come (she was using her pet name), don't you want to catch me? Come follow me and have a nice time." She kept running ahead, laughing until her voice petered out and she vanished as if she had been erased by a duster.

Martina jumped up with a cry and woke up Miss Turner who had been asleep on the other side of the table.

"Yvette, Yvette, girl you come at last!" she said, mistaking Martina for Yvette. Her voice was filled with controlled joy as she rushed to hug Martina, thinking it was Yvette.

"Miss Turner is me Tina. Yvette don't come at all." Martina's plaintive voice halted Miss Turner and caused her to burst into tears.

Martina rushed to hug her. "Miss Turner most likely she get caught by the rain and since it was kind of late she staying over with her friends. She will turn up in the morning." She was trying hard to convince the both of them.

"But when she come how she going to fit in the plan? You think she will agree?" Miss Turner was begging for assurance and confirmation from Martina. She needed that so her troubled mind could rest a little easier; so that the pain clutching at her heart would go away and not throw her into cardiac arrest. Her headache was also worsening and she feared her pressure would soar to the sky.

"Miss Turner leave the worrying to me," Martina begged knowing Miss Turner's medical history. "Member we can't have you in the hospital when we are having this problem, which would be more trouble and a have no one else to help me. Did you take your pills?" Tina knew she was very careful about this but she just had to ask.

"Yes Tina, at my age yuh don't make dat mistake. Is just dat a feel mi heart doing puppalick an' I don't like it."

"Miss Turner come let us go to bed, a will not let Yvette cause you any more problem. Come." She peeped outside again and was rewarded for her effort by the eerie street lights which cast still shadows on the now sleeping houses and the dogs bedded down for the night, dreaming about bones and chasing vehicles.

She steered her towards the bedroom and got into bed beside her. Miss Turner started to pray and Martina listened until her voice petered away into grateful sleep. But sleep proved elusive for Martina, she could not put to bed all the challenges which were clouding her mind and the solutions that evaded her. It would be so easy to become Mr. Tariff's captive and use some of the money to care for Miss Turner and Yvette; but was that her worse judgement speaking, her escapist solution stepping in? She pushed the temptation forever from her mind resolving to hold on to her principles in the face of challenges. She closed her eyes and allowed fatigue and fear to lull her into fitful sleep.

Eleven

Martina sat up in the bed suddenly. Her eyes were unfocused so she rubbed them into full consciousness. She looked around her and realized that she was still in Miss Turner's bed. Miss Turner was tossing and groaning in her sleep, muttering incomprehensibly. She got up and peered at the time, she had overslept. Normally she would have been on her way downtown already. The life changing events of the previous night came flooding back to her just as she opened a window and the sunlight came rushing in uninvited.

Although the challenges and the sunlight were opposite symbols they had one thing in common – appearing uninvited. She peeped through the window and noted that there were no eerie shadows, only stark reality. Yvette had not come home and she was required to present herself at Big Man Tornado's house; the deadline was that night. Uppermost in her mind was Yvette. She wondered if somewhere, somehow, Big Man Tornado was mixed up in her disappearance. It couldn't be that he would want the two sisters at the same time. Yvette was still a minor and even though this was the inner city where different rules applied, as far as she had heard he allowed the girls to be at least sixteen, covering his tracks from the law by claiming consensual relationship within the legal ambits of the law.

She was dragged from her reverie by knocking on the front door. She wondered who it could be and did not respond. Her house had become a regular place for the pounding of doors and reminded her of the porter's scene in 'Macbeth'. Knock, knock, knock. Was it a sound that was summoning her to good news or more hell? It woke Miss Turner and she came into the living room hobbling and yawning with a questioning look in her bleary eyes.

Thud, thud, thud. This time it was accompanied by a voice. "Miss T! Tina! Miss T! Tina! Miss T! Miss T! Miss T, is not police or bad man is only we, we need to talk to yuh now!" There was a hint of frightened urgency in the voice, tinged by desperation.

This was different, Martina thought, it was certainly not an army of people coming to enforce Big Man Tornado's ultimatum. If it were, why was there such perturbation in the voices? She peeped through the window and saw a number of anxious faces waiting impatiently for the door to open, as if the door represented the gateway to some inner sanctuary that would provide answers for them.

She opened the door cautiously, a quarter way, then halfway, at the same time appearing insouciant to the people gathered there. What did they want?

"Miss we just want to talk to Yvette. You can wake her up and tell her we want to talk to her?" another woman requested, pushing her way to the front of a now growing group of people. Martina could hear doors opening around and watched with deepening despair as more and more people edged towards her house.

"Yvette is not here," she answered readily, hoping that would disperse the crowd.

"How you mean she not here?" the lady who had spoken first asked, panic rising in her voice.

Martina was trying to figure out what was happening. Why did they want Yvette? Was she involved in some kind of illegal activity? Was that why she had not come home?

"A think yuh need to tell us what dis is all about." Miss Turner stepped outside, having decided to unearth the problem.

"Miss T a think we better tell you right away what happen. Mi a Karina mother an' Miss Tamlin is Jessica mother." She pointed to the woman who had pushed her way to the front. "Dem don't come home from yesterday evening an' because we know dat dem an' Yvette a friend we come to see if dem down here or if she know where dem gone." Her voice expressed pained hopefulness.

Martina felt a sudden slump in her stomach. Her plan had been to find these same women and ask them if Yvette was at their home but they had saved her the trip by pre-empting her. "A was coming to ask you the same thing." Her composure was quickly becoming a thing of the past.

"Yvette don't come home either and I was coming to ask you the same thing." Her repetition caused a hush over the crowd which had now gathered. Martina heard a sound like someone catching their breath and turned to see Miss Turner with her mouth wide open. A fly could have gone in to investigate, flown out and back again, so fixed was her mouth in that position of shock. A wail, long, piercing and way down in the belly escaped from someone and winged its way into the air, gathered momentum and rose to a screaming crescendo where it was joined by others of similar nature. There were also lower alto and bass tones of unleashed groans and cries.

"Oh God from a did see the big black bat a did know dat something bad an' evilous happen."

"A dog did a hound in front a de yard all night long. Woi dem kidnap dem! Dem rape dem! Dem kill dem! Woi!"

"All t'ree a dem! T'ree is a bad number an' when trouble come it come in t'ree! Oh Father help us to fine dem so we can bury dem!" wailed Karina's mother. "Please don't let dem dash dem weh a bush!"

"Now lady, why you have to think the worse? Dem probably gone off with man or something to have fun. A would still report it but nothing more than dem gone to have a good time." He sounded knowledgeable in his judgement but most people in the crowd did not agree with him.

"It look like you don't listen to the news! You don't hear bout human trafficking an' how dem a sell the young people dem all over the place an' a get big money for it? Whole heap a people mix up in it, big uptown people too!" The woman looked at the bystander as if he had been living under a hole in the ground or had been hibernating and had just surfaced.

"All dat possible," quipped another woman. "Plus dem t'ree little gal was a hang out at the night club round the corner. Dem bruk out whether you believe it or not! The first place you people need to go is round the night club, maybe dem still round there."

"No Miss, no no," interjected a young man. "I know di t'ree a dem an' last night dem have a special t'ing an' I never see none a dem, not one a dem round there, not one!" He was emphatic and looked away from his girlfriend who gave him a look fit to kill.

"Is true," Jenny B, one of the exotic dancers at the club said, supporting his story. "Some new girl come and we didn't dance. I see them there a few times but I didn't see them there last night. In fact Miss P the owner tell them not to come back round there cause police asking all kind a question about underage pickney who them hear say a come to the club."

The argument continued until Martina and Miss Turner went inside, got ready and went with the other women to the police station. She took the opportunity to take three big bags with her. She hoped that with the confusion Big Man Tornado's men had not been watching her or thought anything strange of her many bags.

The police took their statement and promised to start an investigation immediately but Martina could tell from their questions and sceptical looks that they were making light of it. After all this was the inner city and some girls Yvette's age did not see it as anything of great magnitude to elope with men or become part of a prostitution ring. Even though Yvette had become as sullen as a water-soaked cracker and distanced herself a planet apart from them, she was still Martina's little sister and she was desperately hoping that she would be found. Something told her that despite Yvette's new interest, she must have remembered her past forced incestuous relationship involving her father and no doubt shied away from anything of a similar nature. Becoming friends with the wrong persons had destroyed her even more. Now where was she? Martina was not convinced that she was dead but felt she was in trouble wherever she was. She wished that Shimron was there to advise her. She felt so alone but whenever she called or sent him a message he did not respond so she had given up. Since he felt like remaining bitter about her words there was nothing she could do about it. She wished she could summon the confidence to confide in Leonie and Andre but she wanted to overcome on her own merit.

She went downtown and asked Display Board to keep her bags until later in the evening. She agreed readily but eyed the bags suspiciously. "It look like yuh lan', paper an' whole property in these bags. Yuh moving house?"

Martina did not expect her to be so perceptive and thought of telling her a little of her problem but decided against it. "A have to move quickly, you know of any kind of cheap decent place going for rent even if is just one room?"

"No not right now, but a can look around over the weekend, just give mi a little time. You sure something not really wrong?"

"Just a little problem but it soon get sort out." Martina did not look at her but left quickly before she could ask her anything else.

She didn't do good business that day because her mind was preoccupied with Yvette's whereabouts, Shimron's silence and her problem with Big Man Tornado. She spent some time asking her mature buyers if they knew of a place to rent, but she had no luck. She felt like a rabbit which had been turned out of its hole and was running around trying to find a burrow. She had no intention of going back to Port-Herb to become Big Man Tornado's latest conquest.

At the end of the day she still had not found a place. She collected her bags from the concerned Display Board and told her that she would see her the following day but she knew she would not be going back downtown where Big Man Tornado could easily get his men to pick her up. She had no idea what was going to happen but she would not sacrifice herself without a fight. She remembered reading somewhere that if one had an idea that was good it would survive defeat and even survive the victory. Her idea was to disappear before Big Man Tornado could catch her and God would help her to survive.

Miss Turner was waiting for her at a designated spot. She too had a number of bags and had been waiting there since she had made her usual visit to the clinic. It was impossible to see worry lines on Miss Turner's face because of the myriads of wrinkles that resided there, but Martina could see the drawn eyes and the enervated hang of the body. She didn't want her to experience any discomfort and despair on her account but she could not leave her in the house by herself. There was no telling what Big Man Tornado's pawns would do in order to get at her. Her heart jumped in protest at what laid before them that night.

Despite the problem Miss Turner greeted her cheerfully. "Tina is about time yuh get here. A was wondering if yuh catch a flight to foreign an' leave me here alone!"

Martina laughed at the misplaced joke. What a thought! She knew she was only trying to ease the brunt of the pain that was dragging their hearts beneath their soles. "No Miss Turner, you know I wouldn't do that. Even though you shouldn't be, we are in this thing together and we have to find a solution."

"A was thinking Tina that if yuh don't find anywhere we could go down to the little shelter for the night. Even if we don't get a bed we could sit up in a little corner an' have a little covering over our head instead of sleeping on the shop piazza or park which have a whole heap a problem in themself."

Martina knew only too well what she was talking about. She wondered if being abused in the park or on the piazza would be worse than surrendering to Big Man Tornado. Both prospects were daunting so she was glad for Miss Turner's suggestion.

They took a taxi to the shelter. All eyes turned as they exited the taxi; they certainly did not look homeless as their bags were not tattered or torn. Martina ignored the prying stares and her heart dipped as she saw the long line in front of them. No wonder some people preferred to take their chances outdoors. They were not looking for a meal as they had a little food in a bag but they would welcome a place to lean their backs against.

After standing in the line for almost an hour, one of the workers came out and announced that there was no more food and space left. She had seen that coming and told herself that a place in the safety of the verandah would be good for the night. As some of the people went away, she sidled up closer and holding Miss Turner's hand, they forced their way inside. She was not the only person who had the idea and she only just made it inside to get a seat on a long bench. She saved the seat for Miss Turner and settled in a corner, sitting on one bag and piling the others in front of her for protection.

She gave Miss Turner some of the food and saved the rest for the next day. No sooner had she taken out the food than four persons rushed forward, palms outstretched, begging. Miss Turner gave two of them her coco bread and Martina did the same. They gulped down the food like fish on the beach gasping for life-saving breath. Martina was always fascinated with the idea that there were people worse off than she was.

Having eaten, she started to take note of her surroundings. The persons in charge of the home knew that people often slept on the verandah so they left a dim light on so that they could feel safe. Martina was glad for the harsh clanging of the grill which helped to make her feel safer. She looked around and counted about twenty people on the verandah.

Most of them were elderly persons who appeared to be homeless. There were also a few young men who appeared to be out of touch with reality and smelt of ganja and cigarettes. About two of them seemed to be mentally inept and Martina hoped they would not cause any trouble. She no longer felt safe as she looked at the elderly man laughing aloud and rocking himself intermittently. He was talking to the imaginary "Hammond" who although he was laughing, he kept accusing of stealing his hair and hiding it. His childlike face was smeared with black patches and this gave him a clown-like effect. More frightening was a young man who kept smoking a piece of stick and at intervals kept hitting himself with it. His eyes were red and bulging and his hair was matted into dirty locks.

The other occupants seemed harmless enough. There was not much conversation as most persons seemed to be locked into a world of their own pitiful condition. The only voice that could be heard was the pathetic prattling of an old woman relating the story of how she came to be on the road.

"My dear people a had mi decent little house and did have mi good good cook shop making mi living and helping out mi t'ree children. Then the election come and the violence start and dem burn down everything and turn round and run us out of the community. At first we did get a little stay with a friend and then she too had was to run away to the country, the violence was too wicked." She paused for a while as if reflecting on the events.

"Yes it did reach me too and a had was to leave the little one room, Jesus!" This interjection came from one of the other occupants on the verandah.

The lady was not finished with her story so she continued, "After all dat a couldn't get back on mi foot and the children dem get scattered and a lose track a dem. A hear dem gone abroad and yet dem don't even take mi off the street or send even one red cent come give mi. A going to carry dem name to the law and let dem fine dem, wretched ingrate! Eat, sleep, drink, go to school and everywhere else and then leave mi on the street." It was easy to hear the deeply buried pain and bitterness, and imagine the twisted hurt on her face.

Martina had heard similar stories in her short lifetime and could not really envisage how children could treat their parents in such a contemptible manner. The ones who did not help to raise their children were different but those who had laboured to bring up their children deserved to be cared for; children should honour their filial responsibilities.

Other persons started telling their stories and soon she was soothed to sleep by their voices. She had noticed before dozing off that Miss Turner had fallen asleep, her head resting against the wall.

She was awakened by something or someone tugging at the bag on which she sat. At first she did not know what was happening and closed her eyes again, she felt so fatigued. Then a putrid smell assaulted her nostrils and as a reflex, she made a groan and hit out. It connected and somebody cursed under his or her breath. Martina screamed and opened her eyes fully. She saw one of the young men, who had looked unfocused earlier on, standing in front of her with an open knife. Most likely he had not taken a bath in days, he smelt of decaying matter. Fear fortified her with bravery and as she screamed she hit out at him, ignoring the knife. Once, twice, thrice, she struck him in his face and on his hand. Everyone was now fully awake and some joined in the screaming without even being aware of what the problem was. Miss Turner was screaming above everyone else.

The knife fell from the man's hand with a loud clang and as he bent to retrieve it, Martina pounced on him like a wild cat, arms flailing. He came up groaning, knife flashing, shedding a deadly glint in the dim light. Then suddenly he fell backwards as if he had been yanked from behind. Two men had his arms locked and the knife hovered, aimlessly, harmlessly in the air.

"Idiot boy what you a try do to the girl? You mad or what!" a voice shouted roughly.

Somebody kicked him from behind and his knees buckled but the hands held him up, preventing him from falling.

"Give me some way. Move out the way!" someone ordered. A security guard pushed his way through the crowd.

Martina did not even know that there was any guard around. He must have stayed inside all night not paying attention to those outside. Maybe if the perpetrator, whom they were now tying with a rope had known this, he would not have been so quick to attack. Martina watched as they trussed him up in a corner like a discarded sack. He moaned and flapped around like a chicken trying to prevent itself from being slaughtered. His energy spent, he became still like a bird with broken wings.

"Stay there and stew!" the guard shouted at him. "As soon as day light you and the police! Society try to give you a little shelter off the street for a night and yuh come in here with yuh criminality! No wonder some a yuh find yourself on the street! No law and order! And anybody else who try to disrupt the place a going to throw you right outside!" He held up his baton threateningly and shook it all around like some kind of circular dance. Another security guard appeared at the door and he ordered, "Stay inside, a will rest out here."

That is what he should have done in the first place, Martina thought. Maybe all of this could have been avoided. She had felt the inner side of her left hand smarting but she only rubbed it against her side. An urgent stab of pain pulled her attention to it again and she felt it with her right finger. She felt something wet and thick and in alarm she held her hand and walked directly towards the light.

"Tina! Tina!" Miss Turner called anxiously. "Tina where yuh going, is what?"

She did not answer at once as another jolt of pain rocked her. She steadied herself, held up her hand and gasped. There was a long gash on the inside of her hand and it was bleeding, pouring out blood like milk from a downturned tin.

Miss Turner rushed forward but Martina sent her back to watch their possessions. The security guard came over and then called the house mother. She ushered Martina inside and took her into a small room filled with all kinds of bottles and bandages. She did not ask any questions or make any comments but dressed the wound deftly. Martina suspected she had been a nurse, no one without experience could dress and bandage a cut so quickly and neatly.

"You need to get an injection tomorrow," was all she said, motioning her to sit while she went to get water for the painkillers.

Despite the pain she tiptoed to the door and had her first look at the interior of the shelter. As far as she could see she was peering into the female section which had small beds lined out in two rows like an open hospital ward. All the beds were full and in most instances there were two persons on one bed and several small children sharing one bed. There were also people huddled on rugs on the floor. There was no exaggeration, the shelter was really full.

After she had taken the painkillers, she was escorted out. No suggestion was made to squeeze her inside and when she reflected on that she was glad because what would she do with Miss Turner and their possessions?

She didn't sleep much for the rest of the night as the painkillers soon wore off and the pain returned with a vengeance. She bore it as best she could, willing her pain threshhold level to rise. She paced the floor painfully while the guard looked on sympathetically but not saying a word.

Towards dawn, she fell into an unsettled sleep and dreamt that her father had come back and was looking for her but he kept his face hidden, not wanting to reveal himself. Martina woke up suddenly, smiling and joyful but the smile faded immediately when she saw the sleeping street people caught in contorted sleeping positions.

Twelve

It was 3:15 a.m. Shimron turned off his cellular phone and contorted himself like a centipede, changing direction as he moved. It had been like this for most of the night, this turning and thrashing about and in one instance he had kicked Nadra. She had sprung up like one electrified and accused him of kicking her on purpose because he could not get to do it when they were both wide awake. He had asked her pardon, denied her accusation, hissed his teeth rudely and turned his back on her.

The incident did not cause him to settle down, he simply moved as far as he could from her right to the edge of the bed. The time was moving as slowly as an injured person dragging his or her feet along the beach in a measured timely manner. Old Father Time did not like being watched, he only delighted in creeping up unawares and making himself known only after he had made his mark and ravaged the procrastinator. 3:20, 3:30, 3:35, 3:37, Shimron spun around in the bed and fell off, right on his face, splat, like a rotten fruit falling from a tree. His arms and feet splayed out around him like an insect frozen in motion. When he struck the concrete floor, he hit his mouth and the blood rushed out as if it had been in bondage and was now free to flow unencumbered.

He put his hand to his mouth and took it away filled with blood. In panic he rushed to the bathroom, trying not to make any noise to wake Nadra and the baby. He staggered in and held himself up, peering into the small mirror of the medicine chest. He saw the blood, but could not see where it was coming from so he swabbed it with tissue and when the bleeding halted for a while, he saw that he had burst his lower lip and cut his lower gum. He pressed the tissue harder trying to stem the flow and then he felt his teeth one by one, testing to see if any had become dislodged. He was happy when they remained firm under his probing fingers.

He was no doctor but knew he would have to close the opening or he would be left with a wide scar. Right now he had no money for medical bills so he decided to do something he had done once when glass bottle had sliced his ankle: perform his own surgery. He sneaked into the room, removed the needle from the curtain and got white thread. On his way back to the bathroom he almost slipped in the blood on the floor, so he cleaned it up and went back to the bathroom after he had fetched the lighter. He closed the door because if the pain became too excruciating and he bawled out, he didn't want to wake his family. He burnt the needle point and proceeded to sew his lips. He wet his pants and almost fainted but did not stop until he was finished. He told himself he was a big man, born and bred in the inner city where everything was challenging and painful but in order to survive you had to be tough like a stone which had borne the brunt of every mood of the weather and not succumb like loose dirt washed away by constant rain. He had survived a gunshot, he knew what pain was all about so he grounded his teeth and battled it.

The pulsating pain did not stop him from remembering why he could not sleep that night. He was disturbed, troubled to be more truthful about his sisters. At the moment he felt alienated and it was partly his fault. If only he could put away his hurt and anger against Martina. She had called him a pimp, accused him Shimron of trying to sell her, his own sister! That cut deeper than any knife, wounded him more than any gunshot. Tina was his baby sister, and his mother would have expected him to take care of her. He respected her as a person who was somehow different, she had her own values and ideas about life. He loved her for not being a person who gave up easily, just look at how she had achieved academic brilliance against the odds. Even though she had gone and rubbed shoulders with the Joneses because of her father, she had not sat down and griped about falling back to where she had started. Someone had told him only the week before that he had seen her selling downtown. The only thing he had not believed was that she was selling bag juice, not when she had told him that she was selling a product for a business firm downtown. Martina was not a liar so the person had probably mistaken her for someone else. It was not that she was better than anyone else and selling bag juice was not a crime, but that was not his image of his sister who in his mind was born to excel. She was what he would never be; it was not just the intelligence, it was the principles so rare for a person of her social standing.

Talking about principles, yes he wanted a stable family but that didn't say he couldn't have another woman if he could afford it. It was not that he didn't love Nadra, wasn't he living with her? Yet it gave a man a boost to know that another woman found him attractive. He was not involved with anyone else but the temptation was there.

He had seen the text messages and the missed calls from Martina but he was so angry with her that he ignored her and then she had stopped trying to contact him. He was feeling guilty for treating her that way and he knew that she was not to be blamed for him losing his job with Mr. Bentley but he was still angry with her. He didn't know the full story but Martina had accused him and Mr. Bentley had suspended his service, so he suspected that something had gone terribly wrong and he could guess what it was from both their responses to him.

He felt even guiltier when he dreamt that his mother had come to him crying. She was too overcome to tell him what was wrong even though he begged and pleaded with her. She was standing in a yard by herself and then she was suddenly in a crowd of people shouting at someone. She pointed to the crowd and then disappeared into the atmosphere howling and pulling a long black dress behind her. Shimron had woke up shouting "Come back here and tell me! What's the use yuh come and don't tell me?" Nadra had jumped up quickly and turned on the light and the baby had started crying. She took up the baby and hushed him while she looked at him as if he were the ghost he had dreamt about.

He had not told her everything just that his mother had been in a dream he had but would not talk to him. She told him that meant that something was wrong and warned him to be careful as the gang could reach him anywhere, even there. He shrugged his shoulders and told her to stop worrying like an old woman.

It was only when he had called Bibi and she told him what had happened to Yvette and was about to happen to Martina that he felt he knew why his mother had appeared in the dream crying. He was in touch with Bibi using the fictitious name Shawn. He wanted no problem with Nadra so whenever he called her, he would private his number. Also he did not give her his number, he was the one who called her whenever he felt like, especially when he wanted to find out what was happening in Port-Herb. When he called her from the house where he was laying tiles, she was beside herself and lambasted him for not giving her his number when she wanted to talk to him so badly. Something about her tone had riveted his attention and he knew she was not just being a demanding female.

"What so important, yuh getting married?" he had joked.

"Shawn stop yuh rubbish, yuh see the two girl dem dat did live next door to yuh? One disappear and the next one get call to go to Big Man Tornado." She had been excited to be the one giving him this piece of news.

"Which neighbour dem? Member say a had neighbour on the two side." He felt a stab of pain in his head because he knew she was talking about his sisters, but he was playing for time, hoping the pain would not spread to his entire body.

"A didn't even member dat, is not Jaime or Janet, is the two dat live with the old woman dat don't talk much. A t'ink the one dat go to school name Yvette and the very quiet one dat always look serious and help di little pickney dem with the school work name Tina or somet'ing." The excitement in her voice carried over the phone and Shimron felt that she must have been able to hear his heart fighting his chest to escape. He did not answer for a while and she blasted into the phone, "Hello, hello Shawn! Yuh get cut off or what?"

"No man a still here trying to understand what yuh really talking about." He was digging for information and she readily supplied it.

"Yvette and her two friend dem don't come home and nobody don't know what happen to dem. The police looking for dem and the big sister through dem say she bright and she don't mix up and seem not to be in the boyfriend business Big Man Tornado send call her!" The story gushed from her lips like high pressure water from a pipe.

"But why Tornado don't stop! How much woman him one want so?" Shimron had exploded, hissing his teeth. "So what she do, she go to him?" He knew he shouldn't have asked that question because he knew his sister only too well. Big Man Tornado would have to capture her before she would go to him.

"No sir, everybody hear dat she don't make no move and him give her till tonight to present herself. Hey what a stress! Everybody just a wait to see what a go happen!"

That had been one of the times that Shimron had felt like borrowing a gun and shooting someone. The other times were when the gang had come to his house and when they had shot up his house. He felt very protective towards his sisters and knew that as a man he should be protecting them, not being vindictive towards them. He felt useless and ashamed. Maybe Tina had been calling not just to apologize but to tell him what was happening to them. No wonder his mother had been so distraught! Despite Yvette's recalcitrant behaviour she was his baby sister and he had spoken harshly to her only so she would behave herself. Maybe if he had been a better brother she would have been where Martina was.

Where was Martina? He had spoken to Bibi again that night and she had reported that as a result of the confusion with Yvette and the girls' disappearance, Martina and Miss Turner had also disappeared. They had not returned to the house and it was now night. Rumour had it that Big Man Tornado was furious and was blaming his boys for her escape.

Shimron was a product of the inner city and knew the culture only too well. Promising young girls had become

170

ensnared in the grasp of men like Big Man Tornado; they had become chattels in shacks because they never lived with any of them since they had a steady woman or a wife already living with them. Sometimes the women had many disputes among themselves which oftentimes ended in fights. Shimron was often bemused at the women's antics because they rarely got anything out of the relationship for themselves. What were they fighting and quarrelling for when they had already served their purpose and were regularly usurped by new girls? He knew his sister quite well and would have been greatly surprised if she had succumbed to this lifestyle; not ambition-driven Tina!

He wondered where Yvette was and why she had left or allowed herself to be taken away. He thought of her in this manner because of her recent attitude but his mind was deeply troubled. Their mother expected him to take care of the girls and he had failed miserably. Refusing to make it up with Martina was an immature decision. Now he was not certain she would talk to him. He wondered where she was and hoped she was not on the street; that would be the lesser of the two evils but the street had too many dangers for a young girl. He called her, ready to apologize and help, but got no answer after three calls. Maybe her phone battery was dead or she had turned off the phone. If she did not answer by morning he would go searching for her. After he had found her then they would go searching for Yvette. He was certain Tina was just hiding somewhere but what had happened to Yvette was another problem.

The pain in his mouth caused him to ingest two painkillers which drew him into an uncomfortable sleep where he dreamt that his mother was crying again and then she started chasing him with a black belt. He woke up with a scream. It was a good thing he had not gone back to sleep in his bed, but was sitting up in a chair around the table. He knew he was having these dreams because of his guilty conscience and because he had failed his mother. It was four o'clock, the longest night in history would soon end, but he knew it was too early to be searching and he did not know where. He knew definitely that if Martina was reasoning well she would know that somebody would likely spot her downtown and report it to Big Man Tornado. He just hoped that she did not make that mistake. He also had to get her furniture out before it was stolen or somebody destroyed the house. Again he would have to enlist the help of his police friend.

He made himself porridge for breakfast because he could not eat any solid food. As soon as he had eaten he left before Nadra could get up and start asking questions that he could not answer or did not want to answer. He decided that it would be best to search the busy downtown streets first even though he would be jeopardizing his safety. The gang members were everywhere but he just had to find Martina and make things right.

Shimron walked every street he knew with his cap pulled way down over his face and his head often bowed. He peered into stalls, business places and every crowd, but no Tina. He was feeling as tired as an old man who had worked endlessly for years when he remembered something. The person who had told him that he had seen his neighbour selling downtown and had described her, had a particular street and place. He had searched that street already but decided to go back. Maybe somebody there knew her. At the spot the person had described, he saw Display Board and Tattoo Dye who had come back.

He said good morning and started his inquiry. "A looking for the girl that normally sell right here sometimes." He described her and waited for a response.

"A who yuh? A what yuh want with her?" Display Board responded, sizing up Shimron and getting ready to dig her verbal claws into him.

Shimron was shocked and happy at the same time, at least there was someone who knew Tina and was defending her. There was one thing he had learnt in his short life, never quarrel with a female because she could tell you some defamatory things you had never heard before while you were searching for a letter to make a word. No, he would not take this woman on; plead with her gently were the words that came to him. He edged up closer to her, walking sideways like a crab and then said quietly while she watched him, ready to spring and sink her claws in, "A live next door to her and she don't come home last night. A very concern about her and she not answering her phone. Too much bad things happen to these young girls and her family would like to know where she is." He knew he had touched her maternal instincts when he mentioned what was happening to females. He watched as the anger seeped out of her eyes like a dark cloud grudgingly giving way to a white one.

"What is her name?" she questioned Shimron, waiting to tear him to bits if he got it wrong.

"Martina, but everybody call her Tina," Shimron answered promptly, knowing that if he hesitated or seemed unsure her verbal onslaught would rip him to pieces.

"Oh, yuh lucky." She glared at him but with a little less hostility. "A really don't know cause a don't see her from morning. A know she was in some problems cause she had some bag that she ask me to keep an' she was asking bout place to rent." Display Board wondered if she had said too much and glued her lips.

"Oh God a wonda if she fine any place and a wonda what really happening?" he asked, trying to draw what information he could from Display Board.

"A don't know," she said and her bangles shook in affirmation. "She not a talkative girl, but is a nice girl, something different about her." Her bangles jangled in agreement with her again.

"Well t'anks, if she come tell her Shimron looking for her urgently. A trying to get her but she not answering her phone." He walked away sadly not knowing his next move.

"My yute come into mi shop, it don't have neither window nor door, it wide open any time!" yelled a man selling bootleg compact discs. "Cheap, cheap, only a dollar, one bills!"

Shimron moved past him without stopping to look and

he was offended. "Like yuh no hear what mi say. Fire fi yuh waste man!"

Shimron crossed the street and called his boss, informing him that he had a family emergency and could not be at work that day. They were tiling a new plaza and the money was good. He would also be in work for a few weeks. He was standing at a corner trying to determine his next move when he heard two street people talking. They were sitting on their bundles looking tired and hungry. Shimron felt sorry for them.

"A wonder if the police come fi the boy yet?" enquired one of the ladies.

"Dat boy want a good beaten, imagine dat him attack the girl right in the shelter. Suppose he did ever catch her on the street?" the other woman replied.

"Yuh can imagine, right in the shelter! No wonder them don't want them ganja drug head in the shelter," the first one said, hissing her teeth.

"A t'ink we better go roun' the restaurant an' beg some food cause is a long time from now before we get a little food at the shelter." The other woman acquiesced and they started moving off.

Shimron gave them some change which he had in his pocket and immediately their faces were transformed with their wealth. They looked up to heaven and thanked Shimron, moving away and looking at him as if he were an angel. Where the idea came from, he did not know, but he found himself walking towards the shelter. He knew where it was and it would do no harm to pass by and see if Martina had been there. He was not one given to praying much but he prayed that God would let him find her.

When he arrived at the shelter, there was not much activity. The morning feeding session was over and many of the people had left for other places to return later. There were a few people on the verandah, some of whom were asleep or were just sitting there looking idly into space. He walked cautiously towards the verandah, not wanting anyone to think he had come for food. He stood at the grill and peeped in. A security guard saw him and came forward.

"Boss morning, food time done pass. How yuh just a peep peep so like yuh half blind, a who yuh want?" His tone was abrupt, unwelcome.

"Big man a not looking for food, a looking for mi sister. A don't know if she is anywhere here." The pain he had been trying to suppress sprang to his lips, causing the words to come out halting and uncertain.

"Yuh sister? What is her name?" He looked around him as if Shimron were lying.

"Martina and a think she is with Miss Turner, the lady who look after her." While he was talking he was peering onto the veranda and moving around. He suddenly shouted, "Miss Turner, Miss T is really you? Where is Tina?" The elation in his voice was akin to that of a slave who had just received his freedom.

The guard looked from him to Miss Turner and then back again. Miss Turner was sleeping and jumped up at the sound of her name. She disturbed Martina who had been asleep in her lap.

"Is who dat? Is who calling mi?" Her voice was groggy and her vision unfocused as she looked around. She did not realize that it was Shimron, only that the voice sounded familiar.

"Miss Turner a me Shimron and a see Tina with yuh, thank God!" He walked around to where she could see him from her side of the grill. His face broke out in a smile which was very unusual for Shimron.

"Shim a yuh, but how yuh find us here man?" Miss Turner matched Shimron's smile.

"A will tell yuh about it as soon as a get yuh out of here," he remarked, looking at Martina who was just looking on without responding. Shimron could not tell what she was thinking from the expression on her face. He hoped she would not refuse to speak to him or come with him. Well, he was not going to leave the place without the two of them.

"Hi Tina," he said shyly, softly, expecting a rebuff.

"Hi Shimron." She said his whole name without emotion, but at least she had said it.

"Can you come outside so we can talk?" He was not one for many words so he did not want to stay there making small talk.

"Talk about what?" she answered, favouring her left hand.

Shimron's eyes followed her and he saw the bandage. His heart dipped low and a lump leapt into his throat. The security guard was looking on inquisitively for a story of some sort but sister and brother were not the type to discuss their problems in front of strangers.

Martina got up and walked towards the grill, anxious to hear what Shimron had to say but masking her feelings behind a saturnine look. She was glad he was there even though he would never realize it in a million years.

"Yuh certain that yuh want to go out there?" the security guard questioned, wanting to protect the already hurt girl and unhappy that he would be missing out on the story.

"Sure, is my brother," she reassured him. She went outside and away from the inquisitive ears of those on the veranda, robbing them of a story to relate and discuss.

Without preamble Shimron spoke, "Tina a sorry for all that happen. A never mean any harm I was just trying to help out with a job." It came out with a gush fuelled by remorse and relief at seeing his sister.

"Well, a sorry too because a jump to conclusion too quick. A should know you would never do something so low down as that." She just wanted to get it off her mind.

"A come to take yuh away from here. A see yuh in pain so a will call a taxi and move out of here fast, delay is danger for both of us!" He took out his phone while he spoke and started dialing.

"Wait Shim, you sound like you know what is happening with me!" She eyed him curiously and with surprise.

"Yes, active grapevine, but don't worry, you won't have to go back there." He made the call and while he waited he told Martina what he knew and about the dreams featuring their mother.

"But where yuh living Shim and how the space going to work out?" She was anxious about this.

"Well, put it this way, my police friend find a place that is not exactly inner city or big residential area. The rent is more than what I use to pay but the house not join on to anybody house an' it have a big room an' bathroom an' a little kitchen dat the landlord was planning to rent. I don't know why, but from the other day a tell her that a know somebody who might want it an' see how it work out!" He was so happy to help out. He smiled again.

"Lord a hope a can manage the rent," Martina said.

"Don't worry, right now a working," Shimron assured her. "A will help until yuh get back on yuh feet."

Thirteen

It was like almost eight years before when Martina had started attending Milverton High, the top ranked high school located on the hill in an upper class area in St. Andrew. She had been greatly awed by the luxurious houses swanked by high bred, well-kept plants and wide expanses of land which surrounded them. Aunt Indra and her father's house also boasted elements of upper class society, but this house was like a small hotel hidden from prying human eyes except those who extended their necks like giraffes and looked upwards.

The first thing that hit Martina was the utter seclusion of the house, it seemed to have withdrawn itself from society. Except for the opulence, it might have been a monk's habitat designed to make him feel closer to God or heaven. The last house she had passed seemed to be thousands of metres away. She felt she was on the pinnacle of a mountain and could reach her hand up and touch the sky; there was not much limit to reach the sky here in more ways than one.

Martina felt awkward in these surroundings. The towering cedar and mahogany trees held a form of menace attributed to their size and the impression that they were frowning down on everything beneath, except for the three-storey house which rose to challenge them. The other lowly trees such as the pines and ficus were like organized shrubbery to the domineering trees. The shorter plants protected and policed by white picket fences, reminded Martina of cars made insignificant by huge trailers and high buses. The flowering plants were like floral frills or ruffles on wide pieces of green material. The lawns were extensive and went all around the house and were interrupted by the ring road and two out-buildings.

There were two fountains with the spray rushing to catch each other and Martina's face broke out in a shy smile when she saw the pool come alive with a soft quivering light. The tiny folds and ripples of baby blue beckoned invitingly to her. She fought hard to supress the urge to plunge into the water. She wondered if she was still a fast swimmer. She had almost made the national team and everything had flipped upside down. What had happened to all her dreams and aspirations? Would she ever achieve them?

This was a far cry from being downtown even though she was only there as one of the servants in a sense. As she followed the other workers she reminisced on how she had got there. Shimron had taken her to the place he had rented and having made arrangements with the landlady by phone, Martina got the rest of the house to rent. Even though the rent was more than she had been paying before, she was still happy. She would just have to find a job or carry on her enterprise somewhere else. Shimron had promised to help but she did not want him to deplete the little money he had been saving on her account. He was adamant that selling on the street was not for her and was hopeful that a job would become available soon. The plaza he was tiling would soon be opened and the owners would be interviewing potential workers and he was sure that she could get a job there.

She was grateful to her brother for not only helping her to find a place to live, but also helping her to retrieve some of her furniture with the help of the police. Thieves had broken into the house and stolen most of the small appliances but thank God she got back the heavier pieces. The officers had used various tactics to make certain no one had followed them out of the community.

During the second week at her new home she was sitting inside trying to read a book. She felt completely worthless as she was not working. What would she do when her meagre savings was depleted? She agreed with Shimron that at the moment the street was not for her but what else could she do when nobody wanted to employ her? In addition to this, weighing heavily on her mind was Yvette. Every day she called the police for information, but they had none. Yvette had evaporated like steam from a kettle and so had the other girls. The police suspected they had become victims of human trafficking as they had disappeared round about the same time as several girls in the corporate area. The officer in charge of the case said they had a slim lead but facts were lacking. She had listened to another feature on human trafficking. She learnt that trafficking chiefly involved exploitation which took different forms such as prostitution, servitude and forcing victims to commit sex acts for the purpose of making pornographic films. She also learnt that they were sometimes kept in the country or sent abroad. There were many billions of dollars involved so the stakes were high. It was widely suspected that a number of influential people were involved in the trade. This was little comfort to Martina as influential people were difficult to catch and if they were caught it was equally difficult to prove anything against them.

While she had been musing about her sister's disappearance the phone rang. She checked the number first and then answered, it was Display Board. Her antennae was up, now what did she want? She got straight to the point, one of her contacts or links as she called him had told her that interviews would be on at an office in Cross Roads where someone was seeking a companion for an elderly lady who was living in the hills. The woman was fond of literature and wanted someone to read and discuss books with her. The person would also be required to do a few chores for the old lady. Display Board said that even though it was not the best thing for her, it was better than selling in the streets for she was not 'cut out' for that.

Martina discussed it with her family. She wondered if it was another way to get victims for modern day slavery. Shimron asked his police friend about it and he found out it was above board, so she had done the interview and succeeded. This was not the type of job she had in mind for herself, but Miss Turner had said, "Stand on crooked and cut straight" meaning, she should make the best of whatever small job she got, until she got what she wanted.

Well here she was; she had been instructed to take the bus to a point on the hill and then she would be picked up along with three other persons who worked in the house. They were older people who had been working there for some time and seemed friendly enough. Apprehension was tearing at her insides as the van throttled its way up the hill with jerks and spasms like someone afflicted with respitory ailments. Martina had surmised that the vehicle was only used for the helpers and she was correct as when she got to the house she saw four high-end vehicles.

As the car spluttered to a stop, she took note of the large, heavy black gate which opened and closed automatically. One would have a big problem trying to escape from this place. She had no idea why such a thought had entered her mind, but it had; maybe it was the finality with which the gate closed.

She was escorted to a section of the house on the ground floor. She had expected this because stairs were not friends of the elderly and the arthritic. She herself had a bit of acrophobia so the arrangement was very much to her liking. She didn't think her sense of balance was really that off and thought it had something to do with her on and off status.

The section of the house to which she was led did not seem to be part of a household but was a complete suite by itself. Heavy dark furniture characterized by ornate carvings, oriental rugs and what appeared to be genuine paintings were the hallmark of this section. Martina felt as though she were walking through Aunt Indra's living room and expected to meet with a similar sour personality at the end of the walk. The guide was Leonora, whom she later learnt was in charge of all the domestic workers. She had a stolid expression and Martina could not even guess what she was thinking after she surveyed her from head to toe and ordered her to follow in a deep male voice, commanding and full of purpose. Her stride matched her personality, she might have been a soldier leading her troop into battle.

The march ended in a large bedroom almost as large as the living room. An imposing four-poster king-sized bed with trappings of spread, pillows and a confusion of cushions dominated the room, while a matching dresser and a chest of drawers cowered in its wake. An entertainment centre, a book-case a large blue couch, two stuffed chairs and a writing desk were the other pieces of furniture. Martina looked around nervously for the occupant and detected no one.

"Miss Ermine, Miss Ermine, good morning ma'am, a took the young lady to you ma'am," Leonora said, not raising her voice above a normal pitch but the sound spread around the room.

There was no response, only an uneasy silence punctuated

by the light playful snarls of the dogs outside.

"Miss Ermine, Miss Ermine, good morning, is me Nora. A had brought the new girl to see you. She is stood right here with me," Leonora continued, peering anxiously around the room.

"Good God Nora! How many times have I told you not to try and use the Queen's English because you mutilate it so! It is preposterous! Simply speak the way you are accustomed to, it is expected of you!" The irritated voice preceded a black and red wheelchair which rushed urgently from behind the door and came at the two as if it wanted to mow them down. Martina deftly stepped out of the way behind the rebuked Leonora. It braked to a screaming stop and Martina stepped timorously from behind Leonora.

"Miss Ermine, dis is the girl whose come to help you. She will tell you everything you need to know. I will return the usual time with the breakfast." The words escaped from Leonora's mouth in a rush and just as quickly she rushed out but could not help hearing Miss Ermine's response.

"You really do hurt my ears and you are so stubborn! Speak patois do you hear me, not this strange mixture of something!" Her words further chased Leonora out of the room.

Martina watched the fleeing figure, her purposeful tread boldly mocking Miss Ermine's words. Her gaze lingered after her even when she had disappeared; this was a ruse to delay meeting Miss Ermine. Dread filled her being in fear of the sharp censorious comments she had just heard. She wanted to avert her eyes for as long as she could but realized she could not do it all day and a borrowed thought came to her, 'Challenges are what make life interesting and overcoming them is what makes life meaningful'. Well, she was already there and she was going to do the best she could at this job until she found her way out.

She turned to meet the critic in the chair and met a pair of bright, bold, piercing eyes. They stared out of an ageless face with fat, round cheeks which seemed to be glued on to the rest of her somewhat narrow face. Martina had been told that she was seventy years old but her curly black hair denied this. It was the expression of experience, an in-depth or incisive air that really spoke of her age. She had warned time not to touch her face, but it had taken revenge on the rest of her body. Her right hand hung immobile as a pole by her side (how had she manoeuvred the chair so quickly?) and the right foot was stretched out in an abnormal manner. Martina tried not to peer at her too closely because staring was rude at times and could send the wrong signal.

"Well having made your assessment of my person, what is your conclusion?" The voice was curt with a hint of amusement and Martina jumped a little and pulled herself back to the face.

"I'm so sorry, I didn't mean anything. I guess I'm just curious meeting you for the first time." Her voice was apologetic.

"Well I suppose that your response is normal. I was staring at you while I was being stared at so we are equal." She laughed, a small thin sound which rose to a peak and then dropped suddenly and disappeared.

"Again I'm sorry I stared. I am Martina," she offered, pulling out a smile and beaming into her face. Miss Ermine did not give her name and Martina surmised that this was because Leonora had said it more than once.

"Well I hope we get along and that you are not one of those lazy young women who love to dream when they should be working although I don't think there's much around here to do. In addition to reading to me which I hope you can do well, you will clean and tidy up my apartment, wash and iron and fix what I want for lunch." She outlined the duties clearly as if making certain that Martina understood. "And make sure your hand don't touch anything that don't belong to you or else you will end up in prison." She stressed prison as if she had a fervent desire to see her there. "And one more thing, make certain that anything you see and hear here does not become your business, and you will hear and see many things." She paused and looked meaningfully at Martina, willing her to comply with her warning.

Martina felt a slight shiver and attributed it to the strangeness of her surroundings and the bluntness in her employer's voice. Well, she mused, I'm not generally an inquisitive person and I love to listen and certainly observe, but I do not rush into people's business if that's what she is intimating. Making sure her warning had sunk in she commanded, "Read to me from one of those books on the bookcase. Let me hear your reading voice." She sounded as if she were sharpening her ability to make disparaging comments. She had no idea that reading was one of Martina's favourite things to do. There were so many classics and favourites that it was difficult to choose. She finally selected Miguel Street by V.S. Niapaul and opened the book to George and the Pink House. She stood in front of her ready to begin when she waved her to one of the stuffed chairs and pulled up alongside her.

She read the whole story through without any interruptions from Miss Ermine. She made eye contact as she read and realized she was listening with rapt attention. She tried to pretend that she felt nothing but as she read the sections where the women were abused, she detected a hint of anger, but before she could be sure, it was replaced by a tightening of the lips and a firm set of the jaws.

At the end there was a long moment of silence and then a grudging, "Which school did you say you attended?"

"Milverton," she answered simply.

"Milverton! Are you serious? Where do you come from? Why are you not in school? Who are you really?" Miss Ermine reeled off the questions as if she expected her to answer all of them at once.

"Well, Miss Ermine," Martina said with a chuckle, amused. "Yes I did go to Milverton, at the time I was living in the inner city. I am not exactly living there now. I am not in school because I have no money right now. I am working to survive because I have no parents. I hope to apply for some scholarships for next school year and see what happens." She had answered all the questions in a few sentences and she was not prepared to say anymore. After all she was with a total stranger who was not of her ilk. For all she knew, she might be laughing at her dreams; she was only a domestic helper.

That day started a daily routine for two weeks; read to Miss Ermine, wash and iron three days a week, clean and dust her room every day and the whole apartment on a Friday, and fix lunch daily. The washing wasn't much because she had the use of a washing machine and the ironing wasn't much either as there was only Miss Ermine's indoor clothes. She never went anywhere but the doctor and that was only for a monthly visit. Martina settled in and started learning to deal with Miss Ermine's mood swings. She was happy when she was enjoying her literature but afterwards her mood would change and dark clouds formed in her eyes and thunder rumbled in her voice and rain poured from her eyes. She cried about the motor vehicle accident which had rendered her partially crippled. She refused to talk about the accident except to say that she was glad that her daughter had escaped serious injury.

Martina felt as if she were in a different world in Miss Ermine's apartment. Well that was only for the first two weeks. She saw very little of the other occupants of the house save for Miss Ermine's daughter, Ermandine, who occupied most of the house with her husband and two children. A small section was also rented to one of the husband's family members and her two sons. Miss Ermine's daughter was married to Mr. Scalpel, who was in the automobile business. Mrs. Scalpel was the general manager of a supermarket owned jointly by the couple. Mr. Scalpel went out every day but his wife stayed home one day every week. They did not work on Sundays and Martina worked every other Saturday and got Sundays off. She felt as if her whole life was centred on Miss Ermine. She was only formally introduced to Mrs. Scalpel, and the two children, Scasean and Nadrika, aged eighteen and seventeen, she only saw when they rushed in occasionally to see their grandmother. They never spent more than a few minutes and having done their duty escaped under some pretext or the other. Mrs. Scalpel stayed a little longer and talked with her mother. During these talks, Martina withdrew from their presence without being asked. The daughter closely resembled her mother, but she had sad eyes and greying hair. There were times when she looked older than her mother. She often spoke to her mother in whispers which Martina felt was unnecessary as she excused herself as soon as she came in.

The explanation for the disconsolate look soon became evident. One morning in the third week, loud angry voices drifted from the second floor. A bitter quarrel was in progress and each participant seemed to be trying to out scream the other. As the harangue heated up, she could hear each voice distinctly; the thunderous roar of Mr. Scalpel and the tethering descant of Mrs. Scalpel. Mr. Scalpel was prejorative about his wife in general.

"You look like a dinosaur, you do not even know how

to dress properly! Look at you!" screamed Mr. Scalpel.

"And what about you? You are certainly not Mr. Dapper, your belly looks like a pumpkin! You are about to drop a baby!" retorted Mrs. Scalpel.

The next thing that Martina heard was the sound of breaking glass and Mrs. Scalpel shouting, "Let go off me, if you hit me again you coward I'm going straight to the police! You always wait until the children are out of the house because you fear Scasean. You are a coward!"

This was followed by a loud scream and then there was the sound of footsteps ploughing down the stairs accompanied by more screaming. The next thing Martina knew, the door to Miss Ermine's bedroom was forcibly pushed opened like it was being attacked by a battering ram. Mrs. Scalpel hurled into the room and slammed the door loudly, causing it to reverberate as it groaned painfully from the harsh treatment. The house dress she was wearing was torn from one sleeve down to the waist and her left eye was swollen and was in danger of closing out the world. Miss Ermine sat up when she heard the disgruntled wham of the door. She cried out fearfully and struggled to a sitting position. She made it to the edge of the bed and then fell into the wheelchair.

"Nestine! Nessy! Girl you are hurt again! Jesus Christ haven't I told you to go to the police? I'm tired, tired of this!" She swivelled swiftly over to her, while Martina quickly sneaked out of the room discreetly.

Martina was taken by surprise, this palatial mansion was

certainly not a home! This towering edifice so close to the sky with its genuine not pastiche painting, and its mahogany not cedar furniture, this house of moneyed intellectuals was certainly a house of conflict! Moreover, most people were of the opinion that spousal violence was ascribed to lower class people, not to the middle and upper echelons, but she knew better, Stone Cold had taught her that.

This fight was the first of a number of fights and for the most part they occurred when the children were out. The voices would rise out of nowhere, loud and disturbing, to a screaming crescendo punctuated by bouts of fighting. Sometimes she made it to her daughter's room and sometimes she took refuge in the nearest room, locking the door while he pounded on it as if he were drilling a hole. When you saw her later, her flesh-tone skin would be patterned by bruises and angry-looking welts. Dark glasses had become a part of her ensemble whether it was sunny or gloomy.

Martina, even at an earlier age, had tried to fathom why so many women had become so pathetic when it came to how they handled a breakdown in a relationship. As far as she was concerned, if a relationship was over then it was time to move on. In her few years on the planet, she had noticed that a large number of women had remained in abusive relationships citing financial difficulties and claiming that they loved the men or that the men loved them and that was why they battered them. How these women came up with the latter deduction was something beyond logical reasoning. Sometimes they only left when they were being carried out on a stretcher, stiff and silenced forever. She was not really an advocate for women's liberation but she had always felt that someone should educate these women about their rights, especially their right to a voice and their dignity as human beings. It was beyond her why a woman like Mrs. Scalpel with a master's degree and a good income remained in such an abusive relationship. The explanation from the workers that she travelled with that they sometimes made up by nightfall and that Mr. Scalpel sent her flowers and took her out occasionally made no sense to Martina. That man who cast furtive glances at her the two times she had seen him closely, that man with the carved smile that did not reach his eyes, was definitely a sadist, a prime pupil for psycho-analysis. Martina had a depressing feeling deep-down in her stomach. She saw nothing good resulting from Mrs. Scalpel remaining to be scalped.

One morning after she had been there for almost two months, high drama unfolded. The couple was in the middle of a juicy brawl about who had cheated, when, where and with whom, when a black SUV swung through the gate at a drunken angle and Scasean and Nadrika jumped out and headed indoors like all the vicious animals on the planet were at their heels. As they stampeded inside, the first scream saturated with verbal abuse soared in the air.

"Good God that sounds like mom!" Nadrika shouted,

storming up the stairs two at a time.

"Yes it must be and the voice mingled with the scream must be her husband." Scasean bit his lips and leapt past his sister, his face set in a decisive manner.

The couple was so engrossed in their fray that they had not heard the return of the SUV or the firm, purposeful steps of their children. Mr. Scalpel was in the process of administering another stinging slap to his wife when he was yanked from behind. Mrs. Scalpel did not know what was happening but she saw her advantage and sent home a few kicks to her tormentor before fleeing downstairs. Groaning in agony, Mr. Scalpel fought back. Both he and his son had attained the black belt level in karate and they began to fight in earnest. Mr. Scalpel freed himself and ran downstairs with Scasean chasing him like an angry bear. He lumbered into the front yard with only his shorts and socks on. He looked so ridiculous that Martina wanted to laugh but chided herself for wanting to do this on such a sad occasion. The next thing she saw was Mrs. Scalpel running towards the two shouting, "Please stop it you two, don't cause any more trouble! Stop it please!" She was jumping around as if she were in an ant nest.

The gardener and two other workers rushed forward and tried to prevent them from locking horns. They stood in the middle and blocked them, but Mr. Scalpel stepped forward and tried to bulldoze his way through. Height favoured him and he used it to his advantage, but the men held him and he suffered several blows at the same time.

How utterly humiliating, Martina thought, these people were supposed to be the so-called movers and shakers in society, yet here they were fighting in front of the whole world. Heart-felt sobbing from Miss Ermine brought Martina to her chair and she tried to comfort her, hoping good sense would triumph over anger.

In addition to the fights, the couple's children had their own undesirable way of living. They were both heavy smokers and Martina would watch them going out to their vehicle in the morning, their nostrils pouring out smoke like buildings on fire. They did not seem to have even a modicum of respect for their parents or anyone else. They did not only smoke cigarettes but also cannabis. The strong, sickening smell wound its way through the open windows and assaulted their nostrils. Martina thought about her mother and Shimron. Even though they had not enjoyed a good relationship, he would never have smoked in front of his mother. Maybe the children's disrespectful behaviour stemmed from their parents unsavoury behaviour in front of them. One weekend when Martina was working the two had a pool party. Loud music invaded the air, shutting out conversation and impeding the thought process. Miss Ermine looked very upset, but kept her opinion of things to herself. She was suffering in silence and Martina could see the deep lines of permanent pain residing in her eyes. Sometimes when she was truly enjoying a book, her literary criticism was tempered by her embarrassment and emotional pain. The young people not only smoked but also gambled and drank heavily. No one openly reprimanded them.

One morning she was travelling to the house when a discussion about the Scalpels ensued. "Boy, them people a sample," one of the workers remarked. "Can you imagine that after the old lady almost lost her life in the accident cause dem a quarrel in the car and the husband lose control, dem still a quarrel and fight! One a these day somebody a go really get hurt!"

"Trust me is the same thing I always say, somebody really going to get really hurt really soon if they really don't stop! Them really out of control, really! Even the children them, really. The only real sober person in that family is really Miss Ermine and poor thing she really can't do a thing! A hear dat she tell the daughter to leave long time but she really stubborn. Sometimes a really wonder if she really mental or what. Why the wretched woman don't really go about her business? Really man." This came from Pete the gardener and when he paused Martina wondered if he had run out of 'reallies' or did not know where else in his speech to insert them. She supposed they helped him to cement his point. He continued, "A really wonder how the flowers dem manage to grow so pretty with all the bad breath dem breed out on them, really!"

"A wonder if is the big house? Some women love things and vanity more than peace of mind." The first speaker hissed his teeth in consternation. "She have more than enough to start over again, is not like we who poor and a hang on to straw! She too fool fool, a try fight with dat big horse tearing man!"

"She don't see dat him head get knock off a stick! All when this thing which guest (distinguished guest) come up there dem still a fuss," a woman who was sitting close to Martina added.

Martina wanted to laugh in spite of the serious nature of the conversation. If Miss Ermine ever heard this kind of language she would certainly become completely paralyzed.

One afternoon towards the end of the third month, just as Martina was getting ready to leave, the rain started. When it rained at that place, it was as if the house was very close to the clouds so it was closer to the rain and the rain really pelted. It drenched everything in sight and then maliciously penetrated the earth and when it could go no futher, came back to the surface and gathered all the water together and then pushed it down the hill in a gleeful gurgle. Martina watched the rain subduing the plants and felt it was a bit like Mr. Scalpel, arrogant and unheeding. She watched as Miss Ermine slept and felt sorry for her, trapped in her world of useless riches. She hoped the rain would stop soon because she did not want to stay there overnight. This was a daunting prospect as the house did not appeal to her. A knock on the door intruded into her thoughts and she felt happy that someone had come to get her.

"Tina the driver say him cannot drive in all of this rain as the car would be sure to break down so we all have to stay here tonight."

Martina's heart dropped in a depressing manner. She was going to spend the night in this unhappy house! She wanted to protest, but knew it would be as useless as a shout in a high wind. She immediately called home and told them what had happened. Miss Ermine was still sleeping so she did not know where to sleep, but after looking around she decided to settle down in one of the stuffed chairs. Although she was unfocused she forced herself to start reading a novel. She had no idea she was so tired and fell asleep, book in lap like the olden days.

She woke with a start and for a moment did not know where she was. She soon regained her focus and realized she had been awakened by the sound of a vehicle. She looked at the clock, it was after twelve, where had the time gone? Drawn by the sound of a chugging engine, she went to the window, yawning, to see who was just getting in. The vehicle was one that could seat fifteen people, and by the bright light which illuminated the yard she saw a number of young people tumbling out of the vehicle as if they were blind. They did not move away from the vehicle but stood around in a group. From where Martina was standing she could not make out the faces but there was something odd about the group. Instead of talking and joking around as young people would, they stood silent, subdued, unmoving. There seemed to be more females than males.

As she tried to figure out what was happening, three figures came out of the bus. One was definitely Mr. Scalpel, one had his back turned to her and remained that way and the third one turned his face and Martina covered her mouth in shock, hardly daring to breathe. There was no mistaking the face, she had been forced to see it a number of times before her mother had died. What was Yvette's father doing here and what was the connection between Mr. Scalpel and himself? He had disappeared, presumed to be abroad when the police tried to find him for child molestation. What was he doing back here?

The three men had a whispered conversation and then she saw the group of young people groping their way back into the vehicle. They must have responded to an unheard command. Martina counted fifteen of them. The other two men got on, leaving Mr. Scalpel behind. As the bus drove off he walked towards the house. Martina reverted her eyes towards the bus and made a mental note of the licence number. She hastily wrote it down and then stood as if in a trance. After a few minutes she moved and slowly sank into the chair, her head whirling with ideas, like eddying waves stirred up by hard rain.

Fourteen

Yvette finished the dance and stepped off the stage to the sound of loud applause. "Do it again my girl! Do it again! Wicked my girl!"

She gave the audience a bow, smiling as if it were going out of style and she had to get as much of it as she could. She smiled her way pass the catcalls and the hands reaching towards her and the anger grew in her heart, hot and choking. She felt as if she should turn around, summon some strength and like Samson pull down the whole building on them and avenge herself. The stress and strain of this lifestyle was taking its toll on her and she knew that if she did not escape she was going to crack soon. The physical, mental and emotional demands on her over-extended body was too much to bear. She was a helper by day and a dancer by night, and she had no control or say in her life and how to live it. She was a modern day slave, a victim of human trafficking, and she was not the only one. More than half of the girls who worked at the club were slaves. Some of them were prostitutes and some were exotic dancers. She was favoured in that she had not been forced into the sex trade. She could not understand why, as she had been trained for the job and then suddenly she had been told that she would be a household helper by day and a dancer by night. She worked for five nights for the week and this was decided by her unseen boss.

As she changed back into her normal clothes and started having a slight vestige of being human, she started to think about her family and the pain she knew she had caused and was causing them. She pictured Martina working at a job she didn't want to in order to exist and to keep her in school. How had she lost her way and fallen into slavery with shackles so tight that she could hardly move or breathe? The wheel had been reinvented and she was one of the cogs helping to spin it. The middle passage of pain and suffering seemed unending, the waters swirling around her were treacherous, deep and vast; to get to shore would be no easy task.

How had she fallen out of grace with Martina? If she had only listened to her family she would be out flying in the open instead of hitting her wings against a cage trying to stand straight and not succeeding. She had always loved her sister and looked up to her as a role model, someone extraordinary who had achieved academic success because of her perseverance and hard work. She wanted to be like her in some ways but knew she lacked not only the academic brilliance but also the capacity to endure hardship and setbacks. She felt she was not strong mentally as a result of the molestation from her father and how it had caused her to become withdrawn and anti-social. She had become confused at the two set of instructions: "Talk to people, be outgoing, you should not cloak up yourself like that", then when she had found some friends, "Be careful, they are not the right friends for you. They will lead you astray!" She had been duped by her friends' acceptance and their constant encouragement to get with technology and not allow her sister to turn her into an old woman before time. They encouraged her to explore websites which were inappropriate. In addition to that, they had encouraged her to accompany them to watch the exotic dancers at the club near to her house. She didn't really like that kind of dancing but she went along with them because she wanted to be a part of the group. She did not like when they teased her about being a baby and a house rat. Openly defying Martina and the rest of her family had been part of concretizing the relationship with them and showing that she had spunk.

The other thing which had affected her badly was moving from Aunt Indra's house back to the inner city. She had become so accustomed to the better standard of living even though it was at the back of somebody else's house. She knew it was not Martina's fault that they had to leave but she was still angry. She saw herself as being ill-fated, everything had to happen to her. Why couldn't it have happened after she had finished her schooling and had an idea of what she wanted to do with her life? Why did Martina's father have to get himself mixed up in illegal activities and cause her to lose her chance to go to university as she deserved? She missed her mother more than anyone knew. As misdirected as she was about some things, she would have beaten her to a pulp rather than see her go the wrong way.

As she waited to be picked up and taken back to her prison, a mansion in the sky, she looked out the window of the small dressing room. She couldn't see them but she knew they were there, watching like mongooses for chickens, waiting for one of the girls to make a slight move to escape and then they would capture her and beat her into submission, but making sure she was not scarred in obvious places. If the beating went awry, then they would get rid of her like a race horse with a broken leg; she would not be put out to pasture to live out her days. She knew this because Brit-Cara had tried and had been beaten so badly that for days she had seemed more dead than alive and had been seen by the slave owners' private doctors until she recovered physically. Indelible emotional scars, her constant companion, had rendered her mentally incapacitated and she was taken away, no one knew where.

Yvette knew she had to come up with something exceptional and wished she had a brilliant mind like Martina's; hadn't she escaped from a rapist and lived to tell the tale? More than ever she missed her sister and hoped she would see her one day before she died to explain things to her and beg her forgiveness. If she had to continue like this she wished for death, because death was better than some things in this life.

She sat on a chair and leaned against the wall and the

tears came tumbling, hot and tormenting like water from a mineral bath which had a scalding sensation but cooled almost at once. The day she had been captured and taken into slavery (or perhaps she had been sold by her friends who had no idea that they would have been captured too) came rushing back along with the tears. Karina and Jessica had told her they were going to a new teen hangout which had recently opened in one of the uptown areas. It had quickly gained popularity and had become the talk of the whole school. Yvette knew that if she asked Martina she would tell her that she would have to make checks about the place first. She wasn't really on speaking terms with her and she did not want the rational reasoning and preaching so she decided to sneak away. Wasn't that what most teenagers did when they wanted to have fun? Her friends instructed her to take a change of clothes as they wanted to look hot and would change when they got there. They didn't want to arouse any suspicion if Miss Turner should wake up and see her.

As she walked to the arranged spot, her footsteps dragged and a depressing feeling overcame her. She wondered what was happening to her and wondered if it had anything to do with the fact that she had not eaten that morning. She walked on until she got to Karina's home. Karina's mother was not at home so that made it easier to leave. They caught up with Jessica and the three left. Soon Yvette realized that they were not going to the bus stop as they had planned.

"My girl where we going, when since the bus stop move?" she enquired, standing still in the road.

"Lawd my girl you really in a hurry. We a go down by the club go check somebody first. Chances are we might not have to take the bus," Karina informed her as if she had everything planned.

"So how come is just now I hearing about it? Why we can't go by ourselves? What we need them to do?" She somehow did not like the idea.

"Jesus Yvette why you have to worry about everything? Is must you make worry!" Jessica chipped in, her voice filled with rebuke.

"Well my mouth turn cross way and so I will talk when I want to and ask any question I want to when I want to!" Yvette was being her true feisty self.

"Well Miss Inquiry, we reach now so jus' easy yourself and enjoy the little freedom."

Two young men emerged from the club as soon as Jessica made a phone call. They seemed to have been waiting. The two were dressed in skinny pants, through which no air could either go in or escape. They only reached the middle of their buttocks which allowed you to see their shorts and underwear. They wore shirts buttoned right up to the neck. There was something about them that Yvette did not like, and the dyed blue and green and the red and gold hair did nothing to change the way she felt about them. The scars on their faces and the tattooed arms made her want to put a great distance between them.

After joking around with the girls, the men rolled out a black Honda Integra and they all got in. Yvette sat in the back feeling very uncomfortable especially when she looked at the tint on the window. It was midnight black, no one could possibly see inside. The driver also drove like lightning was chasing him and only slowed down when he was blinked in warning of the presence of the police or had to stop at the stoplight.

Yvette was glad when they finally reached the teen hangout and vowed to find her way home when they were ready.

The place was teeming with activity: those who wanted to watch a movie could go to one section; those who wanted to dance could go to the discotheque and those who wanted to shop, or simply meet, greet, talk and date were doing exactly that. Yvette and her friends changed clothes and merged with the crowd. She tried to enjoy herself but found that everywhere she went with her friends, the men were there. She wanted to be on her own, to explore the place for herself, to decide what she wanted to do for herself. It seemed as if the men had read her mind about wanting to leave by herself as they continued to tag them. She was confused because she had not communicated this to the girls.

Then it was time to eat. It was about three o'clock, but no one seemed to have noticed the time or was hungry. The girls ordered what they wanted and one of the men collected the order, while the other one sat at the table.

Yvette wanted to know why he didn't go and help. When the other guy came back with the food, they all started eating and it was not until they were almost finished that he went for the big cups of drink. The girls were thirsty and drank quickly.

About five minutes after drinking, they complained about feeling sleepy. Yvette figured that the day's activities were responsible for this and as she was about to put her head on the table, one of the men suggested that they go to the car. They got in, the three girls at the back and the men seated at the front with amused looks on their faces.

When Yvette awoke, she blinked and sat up suddenly. She felt somnolent, her eyes were heavy and her heartbeat seemed to be fluctuating. She held her head, a drummer had set up his drum inside and was banging away tunelessly, painfully. She felt a scream pushing its way upward and stifled it with a groan. She looked around her but saw only blurs. With a groan she fell to the floor and lay there, dead to the world.

When she awoke the second time she felt a little more focused even though some things were fading in and out like music in a movie. She closed her eyes for about a minute and then opened them again. She staggered to her feet, frightened because she was in an unfamiliar place. There were two other girls apart from her two friends. She wondered how they had got there. As she continued to look around, she realized that they were in a small room which seemed to be in the basement of a house. There were washing machines, a dryer and other covered appliances. What was she doing here and where was this place? In a while it dawned on her that she had been drugged and taken there. Her friends' friends had a plan from the beginning, no wonder they had stuck to them like shadows at the hangout.

She swung around to her friends, anger burning in her eyes and igniting her words. "So this is what you had plan for me! You let yuh friend dem kidnap me!" The anger flared all around; if there had been a match everyone would have caught fire.

"A didn't plan anything with them. A didn't know what they were up to! If I did know you think I would be here now in the same problem with you?" Fear throttled in Jessica's throat, she could hardly speak.

"Yuh always love too much strange man! Love talk to them and show off yourself!" Yvette hit back.

"Even if that is so nobody never force yuh to come out with us, yuh come by yuh own self, so stop blame people, yuh help dig your own grave!"

Her retort was cut short by the opening of a door. All four girls swung towards the sound like a pendulum and quivered in fear as two tall men walked in. They surveyed the trembling girls. The one at the front commanded, "When you hear your name get up and walk straight up those steps." His voice was gruff and threatening, no one would dare disobey him.

Yvette walked up the steps when her name was called. I must be in a dream, she thought. I must have walked through some kind of amulet or some other magical time device. I must be on the slavery auction block. They want to examine me to see if I am fit for the market. Which job will I be suitable for, prostitution, exotic dancer, servant? Who will buy me?

She went up the steps and into a large room with a settee and a large table. There was no one in sight. A voice ordered her to go back downstairs and she did so like a programmed robot. One by one the girls climbed the steps and then down again. They were called upstairs again, blindfolded and the men tied their hands together and hustled them into a vehicle. Yvette could not cry. All around her she heard heart tearing sobs and death wishes. Somebody lurched forward and the vehicle swung for a while, then it stopped. Apparently there was someone riding around the back with them because he knew who had made the move and started hitting her. The cries of pain sounded like Jessica's. Despite her anger at her, Yvette felt her pain and the tears ran silently, swiftly down in compassion for her.

The beating over, they started again. It appeared as if they were going uphill as the air became cool and sharp as the vehicle climbed, shifting gears as it did. When it stopped, she was guided out. She got the impression that she was the only one who was taken off and guided into a building with ferocious dogs whose growls planted fear in her heart and dampened any hope of escape.

The following day, she found herself in a bedroom and

after breakfast a serious young woman came and explained that she would be teaching her to dance and that soon she would be dancing at a club, and starting that day she would be a household helper. She didn't ask any questions, after all what could she do? Her new life began and she was provided with what she needed, but was never given any money or allowed to go anywhere.

As she thought back she convinced herself that she just had to find a way. Martina had found a way out. She was not as intelligent but that did not say she could not think. She put her head down and an idea that she had been playing around with came back to her. She dismissed it as being too dangerous, too many people might get hurt, even she herself. Then the eureka moment happened and without thought she launched into action for what it was worth.

The men were laughing and lunging at two dancers on stage when a piercing scream stabbed the air. Everyone looked towards the sound and the dancers paused momentarily. The scream came again, pealing and urgent and this time a corporeal form accompanied it. They stared as a young girl ran onto the stage, hurled herself to the floor, contorting and writhing her body, holding her heart and screaming in agony. The dancers stopped, mouths agape not knowing what to think or do. In the next few seconds the stage became an area of stampede as everyone pounded to the stage to help the girl. They tried to get her to stand but she flopped in their arms like a soft toy.

"We have to get her to the hospital fast," one man said,

alarm rising in his voice.

"But look she almost dead, she stop breeding and a stiff out. Jesus Christ, it look like is a heart attack she having!"

"Yes cause she a hole up her heart and a scream. Help mi carry her to mi car. A wonder if any police is close by to help us get to the hospital fast?" another man said, lifting her up and looking around.

They carried her off the stage while the proprietor called for more help. The two men carried the almost inert form into the car, and a lady and another patron got into the back with Yvette. The bodyguard who was in charge of the other five dancers who had come with Yvette, charged into action and despite the confusion, gathered the other girls and herded them into the dressing room, locking the door after them. They did not know what to think but one thing they knew, they did not want to be held responsible if any of the other girls went missing in the confusion. The boss would probably take them out literally.

They knew that Yvette was a strange girl in that she hardly spoke and had not adapted to the lifestyle she had been forced into. Moreover one of the bosses seemed very protective towards her and had saved her from the streets. What would they tell him about her illness? They did not even know that she had a heart condition. One man went and made arrangements with one of his cronies and then drove after the speeding vehicle to see what was happening to the girl. She looked as if she would not make it and he wanted to be there to tell it all to him.

Along the way a police car stopped them, investigated, and quickly transferred the girl to their vehicle. When the police car screamed into the hospital compound and over to Accident and Emergency, the porters came running with a stretcher and wheeled Yvette away.

The two patrons of the club along with the bodyguard, waited for an hour before a doctor came out and addressed them. He told them that he had stabilized her somewhat and would do surgery in the morning. He asked for her next of kin's address and telephone number. The bodyguard posed as a cousin and gave his number. When he asked to see Yvette, the doctor told him that she was not allowed to have visitors until further notice. Everyone was then told to leave.

The bodyguard went to his car to make a call. "Yow my youth put me on to bossy quickly." He waited for a while and then said, "Yow bossy, a me Trevone. Boy a really don't know what happen but yuh wah see Yvette sick an' the police rush her to the hospital." He stopped speaking and listened for a while then said, "It look like heart attack boss. You should hear her a scream an' see her a wring up inna pain." He listened again then said, "Yes a know we should a try an' get her to our own doctor but the whole thing happen so fast. A was round the dressing room when she just start scream an' when a try to stop her she give me one push an' then run out on the stage a bawl an' a wring up, an' her eye dem a turn over. Same time people rush on the stage, take her off an' were carrying her to the hospital, but a police vehicle stop them halfway an' take her from them an' carry her to the hospital." He listened again and then said, "The others safe, Gerald a watch them. The doctors asking for family an' a tell them I am her cousin so any information that is available a will get it. This is bad for the programme." He listened again and then hung up and drove away, planning to follow instructions and be at the hospital early the next morning.

He did not notice that a number of vehicles were hurriedly rolling into the hospital and that some important looking men had got out and were striding into the hospital as if their life depended on it.

Yvette was lying in a secluded room in the hospital, not as a patient but as a free human being. She was now one of the most important persons to the police who along with the doctors had lauded her and called her a heroine for the planning and the execution of her master plan. She could sleep freely and she hoped a number of girls would soon be able to do the same too. Right now outside her door there was a plain clothes officer and another one also in close proximity posing as a porter. She envisioned her sister's face when she heard that she was free and had engineered the whole plan herself. Above all she just wanted to be with her family as she had learnt the real value of family.

A few days after Yvette's staged illness, the police like hungry, angry hawks swooped down on different players in the human trafficking industry. They raided some clubs, homes in different corporate and rural areas and broke into some prostitution rings. All this was possible because when Trevone came to visit Yvette, he was cordially invited in to sign a paper authorising the doctors to perform surgery on her and he was arrested along with his companion. They had cracked under the rigid, consistent questioning and had given information about some of the criminals, some of whom the police already had leads on. Two of these were Yvette's father and Big Man Tornado. However, a few of the bigger kingfish were not caught because there was not enough evidence and they had adequately covered their tracks.

Fifteen

"Hi Martina girl, yuh make yourself so scarce a wonder if yuh get rich an' switch? A really had to call yuh, so what's up?" It was Display Board calling to find out about Martina's well-being.

"Hi girl a glad to hear yuh voice. A called you last week and a got voice mail. You are the scarce one." She laughed into the phone, happy to hear Display Board's voice.

"Well my girl how everyt'ing wit' yuh an' the job? A hope dem nah wuk yuh too hard. Yuh is a young girl an' yuh need a break too." She sounded anxious but hopeful.

"To tell you the truth, a trying hard to manage and the old lady is not so bad." She had no intention of telling her what was really happening around her, especially over the phone. She had to pretend that everything was fine.

"My girl, your two friends don't stop come look for yuh. A think dem really interested in yuh especially the young man. A tell them today that yuh not down here anymore an' the boy look like him was going to cry! Guess what?

Him offer me money to tell him where to fine yuh. Him said he will give me whatever a ask for if a only help him to fine yuh. Mi ask him if him see mi look like informer or something a sell. A was ready to curse him but when a look at him face a did feel sorry for him. Tina a t'ink him really have some feeling for yuh. Yuh should try an' talk to him cause good man hard to find these days. Moreover him look good, tall an' handsome." She laughed into the phone, enjoying herself immensely.

"My girl a will sort out that soon. A just don't want anybody to feel sorry for me in the wrong way trust me." She really wanted to talk to Andre and Leonie but pride was her master, she couldn't imagine confessing to them that she was a household helper. As soon as she got news about the scholarships she had applied for she would call them.

"Well Tina a t'ink yuh making a mistake! Anyway yuh have to work out your own salvation. Oh guess what before the little credit finish, yuh remember the man that always sit cross the street, the one who normally come over an' yuh give him food? Is like every day him come looking for yuh. If him could talk, him would talk! An' the funny thing is him don't really beg me money or anything else. Him just looking around an' a know is yuh him looking for. Today a swear a see eye water in him eye. My girl something strange a gwaan! Imagine yuh one have two man a look fi yuh, my girl yuh large!" She laughed uproariously and Martina could just picture her whole body sharing the joke with her in jerks and spasms, and her jewellery jangling and joining in the fun.

"You alright girl, you have nothing to do but laugh at people, continue." She laughed a little and then not getting any response, she figured that her credit was finished.

When she was about to put the phone away it rang again and she recognized Shimron's number. She wondered what was wrong as Shimron hardly called her at work. It had to be something very important that couldn't wait until she got home.

"Yes Shim," she answered. "What's up?"

"I want to know too. My police friend just call me and say as soon as you come home him coming to pick us up to take us somewhere."

"Somewhere where? A don't like the sound of that. That's all him say, somewhere?" She wanted more details, somewhere was just too vague.

"Well dats all him tell me, somewhere, so we just have to wait and see no matter how anxious we feel," Shimron replied.

"A have a feeling it have something to do with Yvette. But why him just don't tell us? You believe is something good?" she asked.

"A really don't know what to think. If she was dead a think he would tell us so a really don't know. Anyway, see you later and don't worry and send up your pressure." He hung up the phone, not wanting to further the speculation.

Martina could hardly concentrate on her duties. More than once Miss Ermine had to ask her if she was alright.

218

Her feelings alternated between hope and expectation, and sadness and disappointment. It was only when she was finishing an essay for Nadrika that she was forced to focus. Miss Ermine had asked her to help her granddaughter with a troublesome English literature essay. Based on Martina's level of analysis during their discussion on books, Miss Ermine had recognized her brilliance. One day, when Nadrika made one of her rare visits to her grandmother and asked her for ideas on a Shakespearian essay she had to do, Miss Ermine had praised Martina's gift of analysis and suggested that Martina help her with the essay. Since that day, she came a little more frequently and this was the third essay. Martina was grateful for the incentive she gave her, but wished she did not have to do her essays for her, that was like cheating the system.

Sergeant Lawes arrived a few minutes after she got home and they left with him telling Miss Turner they had to go somewhere special. By now the weary sun had become wan and drained. The task of bearing down consistently all day had taken its toll. Frail pinkish strawberry clouds mixed with arrogant red were trailing other washed out ones in a nonchalant manner. Pallid yellow rays were battling the assertive twilight which was robbing the streaks of coloured light of their glory by casting a heavy brown pall which choked and almost obscured them. As she watched the unending beauty of nature with the changing of the guard, she felt her life needed to change too. Her light had been dimmed and darkness had set in but she hoped the sun would shine again and obliterate the dark clouds.

The officer drove into the hospital grounds and Martina and Shimron looked in scared silence at each other and then averted their eyes, not wanting the other to detect the trepidation each felt. They exited the vehicle and the officer led the way to a secluded wing of the hospital where a few medical personnel flashed about with brisk determined steps, underlining the fact that a hospital was a place of urgency and purpose. Martina felt like a car being towed because she simply followed the officer helplessly, not knowing where she was going and why she was going wherever. They passed two porters, one seated at a door and the other across the corridor. They seemed to be reading the newspaper, but Martina saw when they cast furtive glances at the trio.

It was only at that point that the officer said, "Well here we are. It was a good thing that I know you Shimron or else we would not have contacted the family so quickly. Not too much talking now." He opened a door and waved them inside but did not join them. "I will call you in fifteen minutes," he said, looking at his watch and then closing the door behind him.

Martina looked around curiously, adjusting her eyes to the half-hearted glare of the light bulb. There was only a single bed in the room, two chairs, a side table and a sink with a cupboard. A ceiling fan made its tireless circuit like the ebbing of the waves. She looked at the bed at the face turned towards her, went closer, stared as if stupefied and emitted a scream of joy. The door flew open immediately in a harsh, hurried squeak and the officer pushed his face in, assured himself that everything was alright and closed the door again.

"Yvette is you girl!" Martina rushed forward, knocking over a chair and grabbing and squeezing her in a tight hug.

"Yvette what a happen girl?" Shimron came and stood over her trying to grasp her hand while Martina was hugging her. He stood as soothing tears streamed down the girls' eyes. He blinked fast and furiously, fighting back the tears. He didn't want them to see him crying. He turned away for a while, composed himself and then looked back at the joyful reunion.

"But Yvette what happened? Girl a so glad to see you." Martina could barely get the words out.

"So glad yuh come back Yvette, yuh feeling pain?" Shimron enquired, watching as Martina disentangled herself, giving him a chance to get closer and take his sister's hand.

"How a should explain it now?" she said, looking up to the ceiling. As if receiving an answer she said haltingly, "The doctors said I have post traumatic syndrome. Is so the words go Tina?"

"Yes Yvette but what caused it?" She examined her face and saw the thin lines of worry and the anxious look and her mind went back to the time when she had been molested and went into herself. Her heart started pumping faster, hoping it had not happened again. Her mental stability had to remain intact. They both sat on her bed while Yvette told them the whole story very slowly, stopping several times to apologize for the trouble she had caused and her negative attitude towards them. She was at the end when the doctor came in with the police officer.

"So the reunion is over. You need to let her rest now." He turned to Martina. "I don't know how much she told you, but we are keeping her a little while for observation to make certain everything is alright."

Martina nodded her understanding and enquired, "Is it alright if we visit her while she is here?"

"The officer will explain everything to you." With that he left, closing the door behind him.

Sergeant Lawes explained that while the doctors were doing their assessment, they were protecting Yvette because she was the one who had helped to break up the ring and could be in danger as some of the major players were still at large. They were keeping her under guard and were contemplating changing a few other things but the discussion was ongoing.

Martina wondered if they were going to put her in the witness protection programme and prayed they wouldn't because that would mean she would not be a part of the family. She did not want any more separation.

That night, Martina felt the happiest she had been in a long time. It was worth seeing Miss Turner's face, the joy and relief were unmistakable, but she felt piqued that she had not been allowed to accompany them to visit Yvette. Martina assured her that she could go with them when next they visited. She went to bed thinking that the only thing she needed right now was to get the scholarships she had applied for and then try to get a part time job while studying. She somehow felt assured that once she started attending university getting a job would be easier. She had no way of knowing that the biggest challenge of her life was yet to come.

Martina walked into Miss Ermine's apartment feeling as if the clouds were about to start breaking up in her life. Before she went to bed Miss Turner had handed her a letter which turned out to be an invitation for a scholarship interview. She was elated and not even the rain which had started to pour on her way to the house could dampen her spirits. She just wanted the day to pass quickly and quietly and one thing was already in place. Mr. Scalpel had left the day before to do business in Negril so the place would be much quieter. In addition, the children had roared off to class, driving too fast in the rain which had come tearing down as if it had a personal vendetta to wreak havoc or cause trouble.

When she got in, Miss Ermine and her daughter were talking. She greeted them and went about doing her chores. Mrs. Scalpel seemed quite relaxed and in no hurry to leave her mother and Martina was glad that at least she was spending some time with her and that her husband was not around to beat and shout at her.

At about lunchtime, Mrs. Scalpel asked Martina to go to the basement for a book she had left down there. She searched but did not find the book at once. She looked on the washing machine, on the dryer and in the open cupboards, but did not find it. She then decided to look behind the machine and there she saw it. As she was retrieving it, she heard a thud and what sounded like a scream and then there was silence. She knew that Mr. Scalpel was not there so she was not really concerned, maybe the helpers were just playing around.

She went into the room and realized that something was different; the wheelchair was overturned and so was the chair that Mrs. Scalpel had been sitting on. She went over to the chair and stubbed her toes against something soft. She looked down and there was Mrs. Scalpel. Next to her was Miss Ermine. There was blood and no movement. She backed away and started screaming, a frightened piercing sound that went up, up, up and could not stop. When she ran out of breath and was about to start again, she heard footsteps, people running and shouting and then the workers stormed in from all directions, frightened looks on their faces and questions on their lips.

Martina could not speak, her fingers did the talking. She did not know what had happened, all she knew was that the women were not moving and there was blood.

The workers dashed in the direction of the fingers.

"Is what she pointing at?"

"Why the chair dem turn over?"

"Is who turn dem over?"

A few more questions and then screams, loud, faltering, shrill, ear-splitting.

"Jesus is Miss Ermine and Miss Scalpel! Dem look dead! Jesus look somebody kill them!"

"Call the police! Call the ambulance! Call God!"

"Miss Ermine get up! Miss Scalpel get up! Somebody call the police and the ambulance! All a yuh stand up there looking frighten. Jesus, judgement come! Call the police!"

It was Martina who eventually called the police and the ambulance. She was too nervous to give a proper account except to tell them that they had to come right away to 30 – 31 Ritz Ridge up in the hills. The ambulance took its time, maybe because of the distance. On arrival, the paramedics found they were still breathing and decided to take them to the hospital. Martina moved out of the apartment before they were carried out, she could not bear to look at them. Who had done such a dastardly act? It would appear as if the person or persons had timed her going to the basement, but who and why?

The police arrived shortly after the ambulance and so did Mrs. Scalpel's children. The latter simply turned around and went to the hospital. The police started their work right away. They cordoned off the room thus declaring it a crime scene. They spent some time in there and then they called all the workers together and the questioning started. One by one each was questioned and dismissed. When Martina's turn came, she went in, fear rendering her almost speechless. Her knees were literally knocking together and she held one hand in the other, folding and unfolding them. They were awash with sweat which had this stealthy attitude of rising up from nowhere uninvited. Martina had all right to be nervous because from the beginning it was obvious that she was the chief suspect.

"Who else work in this apartment besides you?" the officer asked after he had established her name. He had a peculiar way of hanging his mouth open as if to snap up everything in its path. He reminded Martina of a lizard, cold and sneaky, ready to flick out its tongue without notice.

"I am the only one," she responded, trying to sound calm and unaffected by the lizard ready to swallow her.

"Who else comes into the apartment while you are there?" he asked, looking at her knowingly.

"Her daughter and her grandchildren and if anyone else has something to take to her."

"Where were you at the time of the crime?" he asked, bending close to her in an intimidating manner.

"I don't know exactly when the crime took place because I was in the basement. Mrs. Scalpel sent me to find a book and bring it to her and when I was down there I heard the scream." She answered more than she was asked because she wanted the questioning to be done quickly.

In response the officer commented, "You seem to be an

educated person from the way you talk. Where did you go to school and why are you a helper?"

The probe was on. All the private details of her life must be dug out and scrutinized. When she said Milverton, all the eyebrows went up and stayed up. They only came down when she revealed she had to work as a helper as a result of her financial status.

The next question knocked her off guard. "Describe the knife which you use to prepare food for your employer."

"It has a white handle and a broad blade which tapers toward the point."

Again the eyebrows went up at the use of language and were then lowered as the officer held up a bloody knife in his gloved fingers. "Is this the knife?"

Martina examined it as closely as she could and agreed that it was. She cringed at the sight of the blood and fiercely fought back the vomit which threatened to erupt like lava from a volcano. She didn't want to embarrass herself in front of these men who had already condemned her and would take the act of vomiting as a sign of her guilt.

"I'm afraid you have to come to the station with us, Miss." The lizard opened its mouth and snapped it shut.

Martina's head reeled with shock, a sharp pain welled up beneath her breasts and sent needle pricks all over her. Did they really suspect her of committing such a heinous crime? What reason could she possibly have to injure the women? In a tremulous voice she voiced the questions and her plaintive voice caused the officer to look closely at her, but he was accustomed to these deceptive females; not even butter could melt in their mouths, yet they were the evil ones. She must have tried to rob the women or something and then stabbed them when they resisted. At that thought, he asked Martina to hand over her bag. She went to where she had left it and realized it was not in the same position. It had been shifted from one section of the table to the other. She smelled trouble and made to open it but one of the officers grabbed it from her and opened it himself.

"Oh God you have all the money here to pay for university!" he mocked, pulling out some money and two pieces of jewellery.

It was an age old trick, commit the crime and plant the evidence. "I don't know where those came from, they don't belong to me!" Martina eyes almost fell out of her head, her mouth became dry and she swallowed hard, choking back the utter despondency that was threatening to floor her.

"Well Miss, you need to come with me." His voice was calm and emotionless. It was all a part of his day's work, arresting criminals.

Martina felt that all the tears in her had been pressed out. Her lips were salty and cracked and painful to the touch. She crouched in the corner of her prison cell bewildered and dazed. The whole thing was so surreal. She knew that fairy tales were not real, but felt she was locked in one and the outcome would not be "and they lived happily ever after" because she had no prince charming or fairy godmother to free her. The police said they were charging her for malicious and grievous wounding of the ladies and if they died she would be charged for murder. Murder!

She had never really contemplated murdering anyone except Dragon when he had tried to rape her. Why would she try to murder those women? She had nothing against them except for being censorious about Mrs. Scalpel who had made herself a beating stick for her husband. The thought hit her that if they both died, Mr. Scalpel would be thankful to her for getting them out of his life. She would be the scapegoat for whoever wanted to murder them and why?

They had given her one phone call and she had called Miss Turner because when Shimron was at work it was difficult to reach him because of the noisy machines around him. She did not explain anything but asked her to come to the Water Front Police Station immediately. She looked at her cell, it was about eight feet square with one small window. The bars in it were thick and black and so were the bars around the cell. Her bed was a flat concrete block rather like a tomb. The floor was also a grey concrete which appeared to have captured all the greyness of a storm-filled sky. The wall was an indeterminate colour but had also captured the dull drabness of the floor. This is really a lively, interesting place, Martina thought sarcastically.

The clanging of the grill drew her attention away from her dingy residence for the time being. The grim faced warden with his jangling bunch of keys sparked hope. He opened the grill with much fanfare and then shouted in a sonorous voice to the dejected Martina:

"Here is more company for you, more of your kind, wasted humanity, and a burden to taxpayers!"

One of the women he was ushering in spat at him, but he saw it in time and shifted. He pushed the other two women inside and then delivered a resounding slap to her right cheek. She emitted a whelp like a dog in pain and came up spitting again. Everyone hastily moved away and the warder made his escape. He shook his fist at her and remarked disdainfully, "Filth! In here is even too good for you!"

"Is dutty man like you that cause us to be in here!" another woman yelled at his retreating back.

Martina looked at her cellmates with fear in her heart. They gave the impression of having been there before, seasoned offenders. She hoped they were not seasoned in beating up other people. Since she had been confined, some of the stories she had heard about prison had loomed large in her mind. God remember me, she prayed inwardly, remember that I am innocent. Remember that I don't have anyone. I am an orphan and no one in my family has any money. God, please remember me. Don't let them kill me inside here.

The women seemed to know one another and based on the barely there clothing they were wearing, she had an idea why they had been arrested. The good thing for them was that they would not be there for too long because of the kind of charges. She was the one with the wicked charges.

It did not take the women long to see Martina cowering in the corner. She wished she could just go through the concrete and disappear altogether.

"Hey you over there. What you doing?" The speaker was the one who had spat at the warder. The red wig she wore was just right for the proverbial flaming temper. She was giving Martina a searing look as if she were a roach who had invaded her space.

"A jus' sitting here trying to think," she responded calmly, although her heart was drumming out of tune.

"T'ink bout what? What you in here for?' She was advancing while she was talking and Martina could clearly see the T square or cross shaped cut on the left side of her face. Rather than giving her a pious look, it gave her a fierce, bold look. Martina hoped she would not come any closer to her. She made up a charge very quickly because she had heard that if you had committed certain crimes the prisoners would beat you. If she mentioned Miss Ermine, an elderly lady, she would get them mad.

"A had a fight with a woman an' she get injured," Martina lied, hoping she would turn her attention elsewhere.

"Fight, you don't even look like you leave you mother nipple bottle yet! So you a bad gal! You can punch like dis?" She bent over Martina and hit her across the face, right into her left eye and then she followed it up with one to her forehead. This was completely unexpected and Martina fell to the floor, writhing like a centipede, coiling and uncoiling herself.

"Oh God Marla is not you she fight. Why you beat her up like dat? Why you never beat up the policeman when him arrest you or the warder dat box you?"

"Well somebody have to pay for all dat a suffer last night whether dem guilty or not, so don't bother say nothing to me!" She was shouting and spitting anger. "Come a haul an' pull an' a box up people, how a must survive? The four baby father dem not mining the pickney dem an' nobody not employing me cause me not brown nor have edication! Me want dem tell me how a must live!"

"Yes, but is not you one. You a lick the little gal an' she good as have the same problem as we."

Martina could hardly see, the pain was so excruciating. She tasted blood, but did not know where it was coming from, whether her eye or her mouth. She sat for a few minutes trying to block out the voices and the pain. She told herself that if she did not defend herself, she was going to be beaten again and again. She was only in lock-up and already she was feeling it, what if she were convicted, they would certainly pulverize her into mince. With blood and water flowing from her eyes, she went for Cross Face. She bent low and rammed her head into her stomach. Her head connected with something soft and she heard a wail of pain.

The guard who was on his way to the cell shouted into the confusion and opened the grill in a hurry. He called for help as he did so and urgent footsteps came running. They helped the other two women to pull Martina roughly away.

"Scum, scum, scum. What else did I expect! A hog will always be a hog even though you dress it up in white clothes and put jewellery on it!"

Martina did not speak, she only glared at the warder and the baton which he held, ready to beat. He pushed Martina out of the cell and took her to a room. He did not ask for any explanation and she did not offer one. What good reason did a pig have for grunting except that it was born a pig, or a dog for biting other than it was born a dog? Well, he saw her as a societal menace so she would act like one and not disappoint him.

"There is somebody here to see you. Sit at the window and talk through the mesh," he instructed. "You have only a few minutes so make it fast." She sat and saw Shimron. The only person she had ever been happier to see was Yvette after she had escaped slavery.

"Tina what wrong with you? Who beat you up like dat? Is the warder? A wonder if him want to see me turn to badness again?" He was overwrought, his lips were twitching fast and his eyes were blinking nonstop.

"Is alright Shim, don't do anything bad. One person going to prison is enough. Yvette and Miss Turner need somebody and remember your son!" She knew she had little right to preach to Shimron as she had trouble turning the other cheek.

"Tina a know you not guilty. Only God could come down from heaven an' tell me otherwise! A have to find a way to get you out a here. Even if a have to work day an' night to get a lawyer, a going to do it! A must find a way!" The tears coursed down his cheeks, heedlessly, exulting in their release after such a long time.

"But Shim, how did you know about what happened? Who told you? A didn't tell Miss Turner. Is the warder tell you?" She was piling question upon question, something she had always instructed Yvette not to do.

"Tina, oh God embarrassment, it all over the news! A heard it in the taxi coming down an' everyone start commenting an' carry on, glad dat them catch you so quick." He spoke with such pain mingled with tears that Martina started to feel much sorrier for him than for herself. Men did not normally cry, it was devastating to their image and ego but here was her brother trying to make an ocean. "Tina, if you can, tell me everything dat happen, everything!"

Through her tears, she told him her story up to the point when she had been led to the room in which she was talking.

"A don't see how anyone in dem right mind an'

anybody who really know you could believe such a thing! Is only the nice people in this world dat really suffer like this. But it not going to end like this, dem can't send you to prison for something you never do. There must be some justice in this world!"

"Okay Miss, time up!" the warder bellowed as if he were the descendant of a bull. "Sir your time up, you have to come next visiting time."

"A really want to know if she has been charged an' if she can get bail?"

"Talk to the officer at the front," he instructed, ushering him out.

Shimron left, walking quickly, not wanting to look back at his sister. He felt it would have been better if he were the one going to prison. Poor Tina, for someone who tried so hard to be good, why did everything bad have to happen to her? So many criminals were out there running free and an innocent girl was in lock up, suffering. Where was the justice in this world?

Just as she was being escorted from the room, she was taken back abruptly. Martina wondered what could be happening. Surely they would not allow Shimron to come back and it couldn't be Miss Turner because Shimron said he had told her not to come since he was already coming.

"Sit at the window and speak through the mesh," the warder commanded for the second time.

Martina made her way to the window expecting Miss Turner and almost fell off the chair when she saw who her visitor was. She got up to call the warder, but the voice stopped her.

"Sit down Martina. Don't you think it's time for you to stop running from me now? Where can you run to?" Andre Depass stared at her, nailing her to the chair.

Martina was not one to talk much, but neither was she often at a loss for words when she was called upon to speak. She almost missed the chair when she tried to sit and once she was seated she could only stare at him. Then she remembered that her face was a mess and her palm went up quickly to cover her swollen, discoloured eye and cheek.

"Don't bother Tina I have seen it all already. I just want to know who did that to you. Was it the warder? Tell me which one of them."

She had never known him to get angry easily but he was now. Martina looked at him and embarrassment washed over her. She had not wanted to see him when she was a bag juice vendor and now it was even worse when she was on her way to prison. "How did you find me Andre?" she asked, trying to evade his previous question.

"No Tina you first, who did that to you?"

"I was in a cell with three other women and one decided to take out her frustration on me, but I gave her a good buck in her belly. I guess it's the beginning of my other life!" She pushed back the tears, not wanting to cry in front of him.

"Your other life! Don't become hopeless Tina, you are not that type of girl if I remember correctly. I want you to tell me everything that has happened since the last time I saw you. I think it will help me to understand or put things in perspective. But two things first, how did I find you? I heard the news item and you remember Tony Darien? He is in the police force so I called him and he did some calling around and well here I am. Why Tina, why have you been hiding from me? I thought we had a special relationship. All these things did not have to happen if you had only waited until I got back." He was getting angrier and got up to talk. "Now just look at your face!"

Martina just had to clear up something. "I called you after my father disappeared, but you were still abroad and by the time you probably got back things were moving too fast."

"Well, we will talk about that later but I need to hear everything quickly. Tony asked a sergeant a special favour to allow me to talk to you, so I need to hear from you so I can plan the way forward." He stood up and went as closely as he could to the mesh. She told him everything and when she was being evasive he questioned her.

When she was finished, he just stood there looking at her. She was not certain what he was thinking.

"Proud Martina, still full of integrity. I am glad that you did not allow certain things to happen to you, I would have been so disappointed. It isn't what you could have had, but how you get what you have which makes the difference." Some of the anger had gone out of him and he knew he had not made a mistake in believing in her.

"Young man you must leave now. This is against the rules." The warder came forward and frowned at Andre.

"Yes sir just give me a few seconds. Tina what is your brother's number? Give me quickly and by tomorrow I will come back with a lawyer." He put Shimron's number into his phone and then said, "Try to keep away from the violent cell mates because I would hate to start a lawsuit if anyone hits you again." He said this loudly for the warder to hear. He took the bait and looked from him to Martina wondering what such a handsome, decent looking, obviously educated young man wanted with a criminal. He looked at Martina again. She was an attractive girl, but from what he had heard she was guilty as Judas. He shook his head in mock sadness at the young man's retreating back. Well, let him get her out of here! He ushered Martina to an empty cell, and she wished for solitary confinement. It would be better not to have anyone to talk to than to be beaten by vicious women. She knew there was potential danger in being by herself, as based on rumours some of the warders had a less than savoury reputation, but she would fight if she had to. She told herself she would sleep very little and watch most of the time.

Two days later after breakfast, Martina was ushered out. She had taken one look at the bread and some other kind of unidentifiable fare and pushed it aside. She was not hungry; the hunger had been killed by fear and worry.

At about eleven, she was taken back into the room from which she had spoken to Shimron and Andre. She was issued the same instructions as the first time. Her visitors were Shimron, Andre and a lawyer whose name she was told was Mr. Linval Pierce-Grapple. Martina recognized the lawyer's name immediately. He was a criminal lawyer reputed for defending some of the most hardened criminals. He had much clout in the legal fraternity and was instrumental in getting bail for many persons. Martina winced at the implications, so she was a criminal of the deepest dye, what had she done? She wondered if there had been further development. How were Shimron and Andre going to afford such a lawyer?

"Tina yuh good?" Shimron greeted his sister. "A hope nobody else don't fight you again." He scrutinized what he could see of her.

"Tina how are you?" Andre enquired, carrying out the same activity Shimron had. Before she could answer Andre went on, "This is Mr. Pierce-Grapple. He is your lawyer and he is going to get you out of here."

Martina looked more closely at the lawyer. He had a hard, stubborn upper lip which matched the steely glint in his eyes. His sloping hairline added to his harsh aura and Martina envisioned him tearing his opponent apart in court.

"Good morning, Martina is it?" he asked, trying to smile.

"Yes it is, Martina Patterson."

"Ms. Patterson I want you to tell me everything that happened. Don't leave anything out, more than all, tell me the truth. If I don't know the truth I won't be able to make a good case to defend you." He gave her a look which was meant to be encouraging, but at the same time it had a hint of warning in it.

Martina thought that her story was so simple that there was nothing to lie about, so she told it just as it had happened.

"Yes sir, that is all," she said with finality.

"Tell me, does the apartment door open into the rest of the house on that floor, and is it always kept open?"

"Yes sir, only a door separates the apartment. When I come through in the mornings I only close the door not lock it with a key. Anyone who has anything to do in the apartment normally just knock and come right in."

"And the knife, where do you always leave it?" His eyes matched the glint of a knife as he continued the questioning.

"On the table where I use it to prepare her lunch," she responded.

"They found some jewellery in your bag. Have you ever seen those pieces of jewellery before?"

"Yes ever since I went there they were just lying on the dresser. Maybe they gave her hope or reminded her of better days."

Mr. Pierce-Grapple looked at Martina closely. He was impressed by the girl's tone, language and demeanour. He made a mental note of everything, there was somebody who would be interested in hearing about this. "Well I have put in an application for bail and I have the hearing in fifteen minutes. Don't bother yourself, before you know it you will be out of here because some things just do not add up." He left abruptly, striding out importantly with his attaché swinging swiftly to match his gait.

Shimron and Andre remained, chatting about anything and everything, trying to boost Martina's spirit. They left a few minutes later when the warder ordered them out. They promised they would be back soon to take her home.

She felt hope burgeoning within her. Caution warned her to snuff out this hope but she told herself she would keep it alive even a little to chase away depression. She did not want to have a nervous breakdown or become afflicted with mental problems. Most of her life had been filled with challenges and she had only tasted a better life when her father had stepped in and that had vanished as if it had never been. She had to keep her hope alive or be crushed by her adversities. She willed herself to have courage and was reminded of a thought she had once stumbled on, 'Courage is to never let your actions be influenced by your fear'. They had taken her fingerprints, photographed her from all angles, accused her and hit her, but God would deliver her out of this nightmare, fear would never defeat her.

Hunger and anxiety must have driven her to sleep. The hard, cold concrete which squeezed and tortured her back and sides had been ignored as sleep induced her senses, cajoling her into forgetfulness. She awoke and sat up suddenly, disoriented at first and then only too soon reality plunged in, reminding her where she was and bringing her ordeal forcibly to her. She heard the clatter and clanging of the grill and immediately stood up. She liked being on her feet whenever anyone entered because she did not know what the person was up to or if she would be getting new 'friends'. It was a warder, a female she had never seen before. She regarded her warily, moving towards the back of the cell. They looked at each other suspiciously.

"Follow me," she said, holding the grill open for Martina.

She did as she was told, wondering if they were going to relocate her. She hoped it would not be some faraway place where no one would hear her scream if she had to. She followed the warder, past the now familiar visitors' room, past some cells where the women shouted at her and yelled obscenities at the warder, past some other rooms in which people were either talking on the phone or working at desks, and right to the front where Mr. Pierce-Grapple, Andre, Shimron, Miss Turner and Yvette were waiting for her. They all started to laugh and cheer and Martina, feeling a rush of freedom even if it was only for a while, stormed towards them, unchecked tears racing down her face in wild abandon as she hugged and was hugged by everyone.

Sixteen

Martina ushered the client into the lawyer's office and then went back to her job of making notes from a folder which Mr. Pierce-Grapple's secretary had given her. She was doing a few weeks of holiday work at the office while waiting for the first hearing of her case. It was the middle of June and she was wishing with her whole life that the lawyer would have some definite words for her by the beginning of August so that she would know what direction her life would take. She did not want to bother Mr. Pierce-Grapple with questions knowing that he was a very busy man. She reasoned that he must be making millions by the month because of the number of cases he had taken unto himself.

There were two things on her mind: would Mrs. Scalpel and Miss Ermine ever recover and be able to tell the truth about who had inflicted the injuries and tried to frame her? Would the university accept her with prison looming over her head? She had gone for the first scholarship interview and she told herself she had done well enough, but she did not like the large number of personal questions which they had asked. They seemed more interested in what had happened to her since she deferred the offer the first time and how she had become entangled with the law. Her presumed criminal act had preceded her and she felt they were holding it against her. She was guilty until proven innocent! She did not have much hope and had started applying to some offshore universities just in case. She knew they were more expensive but she had to try something. When she told Andre, he had chided her for being too hasty.

"Tina I know it looks bad but believe me things will work out. All those people who are turning up their noses in distaste will soon know the truth. I know it will not remain hidden for long."

Leonie had expressed the same sentiments. "Tina I have a feeling that there is going to be a breakthrough somehow and I don't mean years down the line. Something has to give."

The first hearing did not come through because the prosecution had not even begun to prepare its case as yet. They are fiddling while Rome is burning, Martina thought. My future is on hold all because of a real criminal. If she had not seen Mr. Scalpel drive out the day before the murder he would be her chief suspect. Who else would want the ladies dead? There was no perfect crime, if the police were not so certain it was an open and shut case they would have done some investigation to try and find out the truth. She was almost ready to sink into despondency but her friends encouraged her to believe that life was worth living and there would be a way, and that thought would help to create the fact.

When she went to work a week later, the office was teeming with people. There were several police officers and some other people who Martina could not associate with any particular group. She felt that everything was finished for her, maybe one of the ladies had died and they had come to arrest her again. She would have run through the door to a place unnamed but there were people all around so she fled to the bathroom hoping that no one had noticed she had turned up for work. She could not call her friends and family because she did not want them to find out too quickly what she supposed had happened. It was strange that she thought of her parents at that time. They would most certainly turn in their graves. She thought of her family on her father's side, no one except Tian had tried to contact her and he was not even in the country. She was standing in the shower area when she heard her name being called. She did not respond.

"Martina, the boss wants you in the office right now. I know you are somewhere in here because somebody saw you come in. Why are you hiding? What is the problem?" It was the secretary but Martina did not move. "Come on Ms. Patterson, you know Mr. Pierce-Grapple is a very serious and busy man and he has no time to waste."

Martina came out silently, trying to hold her head high. What was to be must be. She would have to face her fate. "Well here I am. I will even go before you," she said resignedly.

"I don't know what is happening to you, but I am certain you must have a good reason for behaving this way." She gave Martina a quizzical look and followed her.

Martina wanted to know how she knew where she was and then she remembered that there was a surveillance camera in the building and once you came in you would be picked up. They must have been laughing at her scornfully!

She followed the secretary into a room which she had never been in before. There were four persons in it including her lawyer. Why did they have to gather to tell her that she would be arrested again? Why didn't they just do it instead of calling the whole world to witness it?

"Sit down Ms. Patterson," invited the only female among the four, trying to smile.

Ms. Patterson and trying to smile, who did she think she was, Matlock, sending you to prison and smiling with you at the same time? Why was Mr. Pierce-Grapple allowing them to talk to her, wasn't he her lawyer?

"Ms. Patterson," she continued, "we are here to give you some information." She looked Martina straight in the eyes.

Well, Martina thought, cut out the preamble and inform me. I do not like looking into your deceptive eyes.

"We would like to tell you that the charges have been dropped."

Martina stared at her in an incomprehensible manner. What was she talking about? Her face registered her stupefied state of mind. She just stared at her. All the words that she had ever known had been erased from her mind, wiped out, obliterated!

"Ms. Patterson are you understanding me?" the lady questioned, staring at the dumb girl.

"Martina, Miss Nugent is telling you that you are no longer being held responsible for the injuries sustained by Mrs. Scalpel and her mother," Mr. Pierce-Grapple tried to explain.

"How, how, how is this possible?" Martina tried to summon her departed vocabulary.

"Let me explain," Ms. Nugent replied. "Following your arrest your family was fortunate to have retained Mr. Pierce-Grapple here as your lawyer. He along with one of the police officers assigned to the case, did not think certain things added up. For example, there were no prints on the money, yours or anyone else's. The knives had your prints, but then you were the only person who was using it. Although it had blood on it, it was not the murder weapon because it was short and dull and the wounds inflicted were made by a much longer, sharper knife. In addition to that, the experts determined that the wounds had been inflicted by a left-handed person who is much stronger and taller than you are." She paused and looked at Martina, whose mouth was wide open.

"Are you here at all Miss?" one of the gentlemen asked, looking at Martina as if she had morphed into something from another planet.

"You would never believe it," Mr. Pierce-Grapple supplied, "but Ms. Patterson is one of the most intelligent young women you'll ever meet and quite eloquent too. I think she is just at a loss for words at the turn of events. One minute she is headed straight for prison and the next she has been exonerated." He gave Martina a warm, encouraging smile.

"Mr. Pierce-Grapple is so correct," Martina said, feeling as if her vocabulary had been replenished. "I am just so shocked at the sudden turn of events. I came in here expecting to be hauled off to prison, not to be told I can breathe freely again." She shook her head in bewilderment.

"Well, the story is not over as yet," the gentleman who had spoken continued. "You will be glad to know that the old lady has regained consciousness, her wounds were fewer in number than her daughter. She was able to speak and told us what happened."

"Miss Ermine is still alive, thank God!" Martina broke out. "Can I visit her?"

"You seem to like her," the gentleman who had not spoken before observed.

"Yes she has her ways, as we all do, but she has an intelligent, analytical mind and most of all she is not a snob, not to me at least. I suppose I spoke her literary language and so we had some good reading and discussion sessions."

"So you were not just a helper to her?" Miss Nugent enquired, amazed.

"I was actually employed to read to her and then other chores were added," Martina explained.

"Well, back to my story," the gentleman continued.

"She told us that as soon as you left the room Mr. Scalpel rushed in–"

"Mr. Scalpel! But he went away the day before the incident!" Martina could not help interrupting.

"Yes but apparently he had not gone far. You do know the house has an internal monitoring system so everyone who comes in and goes out is seen." He did not wait for a response but continued. "You might not have known, but in the nights different security guards work at the house. The company said they were told not to send anyone that night. It was Mr. Scalpel who came in dressed as the security guard and because the house is so big he was able to hide without anyone knowing he was there. As soon as you went to the basement he came in and started his evil deed. They were completely taken by surprise. He meant to kill them so he did not even disguise himself. He did not calculate on them living. He also turned off the security system prior to his deed so that whole section is missing but we have Miss Ermine's statement. There was longstanding abuse over the years but his wife did not report him. He decided to get rid of her because she discovered that he was involved in human trafficking and threatened to go to the police if he did not stop abusing her. Mr. Scalpel was raised in an abusive home so he knew no other way and was not about to stop."

There was silence at the end of the account. To Martina, the whole thing had been surreal from the beginning. She thought of the execrable Mr. Scalpel whom she barely knew, but who had decided to end her dream and aspiration and her life. She felt no remorse at the fact that he would be going to prison and hoped he would remain there forever. It was her fervent prayer that the women would survive and Mrs. Scalpel would have learnt something about putting one's self above pride and money. The thought came to Martina that 'we all make mistakes, but we should all be wary in how willing we are to admit to them and make amends'.

Seventeen

Martina dropped her pen on the desk with a clatter and a smile on her face. This marked the end of her second year examination specializing in media and communication. This final paper meant that she was free for the next two and a half months and could spend more time working money for next term and spending more time with her family.

As she waited for the papers to be collected, memories of her first day at university came flowing back to her. She had alighted from the taxi at Marvin Hall's gate. Her legs were engaged in a wobbly dance with music supplied from the staccato beat of her heart. It was gasping and spluttering like a pipe whose supply of water was inconsistent. If her knapsack had not been anchored to her back, it would have provided a refuge for her sweating palms, a place to grip and prevent her tremulous fingers from folding and unfolding. The road ahead of her though short, seemed interminable and forbidden despite the large number of students who were walking before and behind her laughing and chattering like carefree birds heralding the coming of a new day.

For her it was a new day, one she had dreamt continuously about; now that she was there apprehension clutched at her being, beating down the optimism that she had mustered since she had accepted the second invitation to study for a Bachelor's Degree in media and communication. Her nerves were taut and anxiety threatened to unglue her resolve. What was she nervous about when everybody else appeared excited and expectant like Christmas was near and presents were forthcoming? She was fearful that they would recognize her as the girl who had been accused of murder. Although the charges had been dropped there was a stigma attached to anyone who had ever been accused of anything dishonest.

It had not been easy for Martina. After the dismissal of her case, she had done another interview for a scholarship, but in the end only one scholarship had come through. It was not enough to cover everything so the lawyer had signed as a guarantor for her to get a student's loan. In addition to that, she worked at his office on Tuesdays and Fridays when she had a light timetable and on Saturdays. It was really frenetic but she had stuck with it. She had even made time on Thursdays for clubs – debating and swimming. She had taken up swimming seriously again, practising on the afternoons when she was not working. To her it was not the competitiveness which really mattered, but the totally relaxing and exhilarating feeling it gave her. She was fast and did well at different strokes and the coach was watching her for the national team but Martina was more interested in getting top grades than excelling in swimming.

The first year of university had been a mixed one. She remembered vividly unfriendly stares and evasive looks as she was pointed out by students she had known at Milverton. Even though she had been exonerated from the crime before she even set foot in the university, some people still behaved as though she were a criminal. Not only this, but her father's yet unproven crime was further used to label her.

One girl had the temerity to ask her how she had managed to get into university with her prison record. Andre and Leonie had been her rock; real, authentic, friends. Martina thrived on their encouragement and friendship. There was a particular girl who was interested in Andre and had taken him to task about his friendship with Martina, a girl from the inner city who had tasted of prison. Andre had told her that girls with true integrity and brilliance who were not prepared to be used by anyone, were gems and were worth him and better any day of the week. She had looked at him in shock and thereafter had avoided the couple like a terminal illness.

Martina had stilled many of her critics at the end of the first semester's examination by not only topping the grades in her faculty, but also tying with a male in the university with the highest grade point average. Her family and friends were elated and she got the green-eyed as well as the admiring glares. In all of this she remained calm and kept her focus, counting every cent so that it could cover her daily needs. She refused help from Andre, telling him he had done more than enough by helping out with the lawyer to save her from prison. When she mentioned Mr. Pierce-Grapple, Andre told her that all he had done was hire him.

"What do you mean all you have done was to hire him?" Her voice was querulous, she just did not understand.

"That's exactly what I mean Tina, I hired him and when it was time to settle the account, he told me that it was already settled and he refused to tell me by whom. When I asked Shimron if he knew who had done it, he too had no idea."

She did not want to ask Mr. Pierce-Grapple, but she intended to find out. She felt he had not done a work of charity and she wondered how he had just given her a job at his office without her asking him. She wondered if Miss Ermine had anything to do with it as she had questioned her about her welfare when she went to visit her.

It was in the middle of the term when she was summoned to the vice chancellor's office. Knowing that trouble always sought her out, she was very nervous. She didn't think he wanted to congratulate her for keeping her high grade point average for the second year running, because there had already been an award ceremony for that. What had she done? Did it have anything to do with her father? Had they found his remains or something? The secretary ushered her into the office and told her to sit and await the vice chancellor. She sat nervously, but set her face like flint, ready to deal with whatever came.

The vice chancellor walked into the office with a smile that covered his whole face and extended beyond his face to his bald head. He walked towards her and extended his hand. Uncertainly, hesitantly, she shook it and then looked strangely at him, her face a big question mark.

"Ms. Patterson, so we meet again. You have done yourself and this university proud! You have over-ridden the odds and risen above the tsunamis in your life. I congratulate you on being selected as this year's Rhode Scholar!" His smile got so wide it fell off his face.

"I am what?" Martina asked in a whisper then shouted, "Oh my God! Oh my God! Thank you Lord!" She stopped shouting and covered her face. "Sorry sir, this is so surprising! I must be dreaming!"

"No you are not and it is only human to act the way you have done. Congratulations again and here is your letter of award. We will keep you posted on your schedule from now on; you know interviews, talks, the whole works. Just keep humble, you are an inspiration to all those who have held their heads high despite poverty and adversity. You will inspire others and encourage them with a view of how far they have come and how far they can go."

Martina felt as if she were flying. She had seen the advertisement for the scholarship and had applied. She had asked one of her lecturers to write a recommendation for her and she had asked her a large number of questions about herself before doing so. She had not really expected to be considered after the interview, but here she was, the winner.

She called Andre, Leonie, her family and Mr. Pierce-Grapple to inform them of the good news, not knowing that the news of her life story was all over the media and the Internet.

"Tina will we still be your friends? Can you still talk to commoners like us?" Andre joked later, hugging Martina. She knew it was just a joke because she had agreed to marry him as soon as he had finished his bar examination.

"Tina girl will you still remember us when you go to Oxford University?" Leonie asked, tears streaming down her face. She was so happy for her friend, so glad she had not given up on her and had believed in her integrity and honesty.

When she got home, the door was closed and silence greeted her. She wondered where everyone was when she just wanted to hug them and cry. As she stood there a vehicle containing Shimron, Yvette and Miss Turner drove up. They commanded Martina to get in. She asked them where they were taking her, but they only laughed and hugged and congratulated her. Miss Turner and Yvette cried while Martina explained the scholarship.

They arrived at Mr. Pierce-Grapple's office and when the doors were opened, the lawyer, his family, Andre, the whole staff and some other people that Martina did not know all shouted, "Surprise! Congratulations!" The office had been transformed into a celebration centre with balloons, flowers, a banner with a celebratory message and food.

At the end of the celebrations Mr. Pierce-Grapple steered Martina away from the crowd. He led her to the half-lit room where she had received the glorious news of her release from the charge. Now what was he up to again? Martina looked at him hoping to get an answer.

"Martina do you remember this man?" Mr. Pierce-Grapple asked, turning on the light.

She jumped back, almost running back through the door. This must be a joke! She hadn't summed up the lawyer as someone who made shocking jokes and yet this must be a joke! Seated at the table with his face lifted to her was the man she had always fed downtown. The same man with the taut face who always sat across the road from her and who had guided her the day when the melee had taken place.

"Yes sir I remember him but who is he? Why is he here?" As she looked, the man pulled off his hat and pulled a mask from his face. Martina gave a gasp like one struggling to breathe and then she rushed towards him, almost falling over in her shock and joy. "I always wanted to believe you were not dead! My father you always turn up in strange ways in my life!" She ran into his open arms, hugging him for the second time in her life; the first had been when she had passed her CAPE subjects.

"But how and why were you downtown in this disguise and why didn't you answer my calls or even give me an indication that you were alive?" She drew back from him, examining him. His hair was dusted with grey and he looked a little older and drawn, but he was still her handsome father, Martin Patterson.

"I think I can answer some of those questions while he is enjoying the moment," the lawyer replied, laughing. "Your father and I go back a long time to high school and university. When his trouble started, he came to me and we decided on this plan. I have never told anyone his whereabouts, but I set out to investigate the company and all the problems. When I had enough evidence I went to the Commissioner and presented it to him. He too started an investigation. We now have enough evidence to clear your father's name." He stopped and looked from daughter to father. "Your father had lost everything and all his assets were frozen so he was just as poor as everyone else. I had a secret place for him but decided the best daytime place was right under the police's nose in disguise. No one would ever think of looking for him in plain view." He paused and Mr. Patterson took up the story.

"When I saw you selling downtown, it broke my heart and I almost had a nervous breakdown but my friend here helped me. I became your watchman and followed you all over town to make certain you were alright. When we secretly checked Aunt Indra to find out what had happened, she said you just left suddenly without any explanation. I knew she was lying as I had always known she was snobbish. It was a pity she might never know how you have crossed your rivers." Mr. Patterson's tone changed and Martina looked more closely at him. There was another sadness besides the main one which had changed his life forever.

"What is it?" she questioned. "Is something wrong with her?" Even though Aunt Indra had denigrated, lambasted and cast her to the wind, she was not eager to hear that anything bad had befallen her.

"Well, she had a bit of misfortune. About two months ago, she was outside tending her plants when thieves crept up on her. I don't know what happened to the dogs as I learnt they did not alert her of the thieves' presence. They took her inside, tied her up and robbed the place. Sometime during this, she suffered a heart attack. She is still in the hospital but it will only be a matter of time. I understand that her children and grandchildren are at the house now."

Mr. Pierce-Grapple continued the story. "We even knew where you were living at first and where you are living presently, there are ways and means."

"Yes we did, but as I said I could not help you. I was lucky to escape with my life but I will make a new start. My house was vandalized because my family has stayed away. I will find a way to start over when everything is cleared up and they have released my assets. Most of it will go into paying bills. I also owe my friend here money for your case."

So that was it, Martina thought. She now knew how her

fees had been paid. She felt deep gratitude and thanked him again. She was happy that it had not been Andre. Even though they had decided to get married as soon as he finished his bar examination, she did not want to feel as if she were beholden to him.

Martina cried for the last time that day. God had been so good to her. Her father would find a way just as she had. The thought came to her, 'everyone who got where he is, had to begin where he was'.

Rivers, no matter how deep they were, would always part like the Red Sea and the embattled swimmer would cross to the other side, holding up the rod triumphantly.